The Seven Poor Travellers

The Seven Poor Travellers

Charles Dickens

with
George A. Sala
Adelaide Anne Procter
Wilkie Collins
Eliza Lynn Linton

Edited by
Melisa Klimaszewski

Hesperus Classics

Hesperus Classics
Published by Hesperus Press Limited
4 Rickett Street, London SW6 1RU
www.hesperuspress.com

First published in *Household Words* in 1854
First published by Hesperus Press Limited, 2010

This edition edited by Melisa Klimaszewski
Introduction, notes, and note on the text © Melisa Klimaszewski, 2010

Designed and typeset by Fraser Muggeridge studio
Printed in Jordan by Jordan National Press

ISBN: 978-1-84391-206-4

CONTENTS

INTRODUCTION

Having written four successful annual Christmas issues of his journal *Household Words*, Charles Dickens set out with a new plan for the 1854 collection of stories. Rather than continue with the loose concept of *A Round of Stories by the Christmas Fire*, which had served so well in 1852 that Dickens repeated it in 1853 with *Another Round of Stories by the Christmas Fire*, he enhanced the idea. For the first time, Dickens devised a full tale and theme to frame and unite the stories in the Christmas number. Creating a mini-plot with a traveller arriving at an almshouse and donating a Christmas Eve dinner to its residents, Dickens enriched the environment in which the tales were told. Although the two *Round of Stories* numbers included some descriptions of the narrators and even direct exchanges between some of them, few passages linked the stories, and the label 'round' invited repetition and overlap between the tales. In writing a more structured frame tale for *The Seven Poor Travellers*, Dickens deployed a narrative strategy to which he would return for over a decade as he strung together stories for the holiday season.

The stories in this collection are as randomly assorted as the people one would suddenly discover at an almshouse, so the frame concept does create a sort of logic that holds them together convincingly. Dickens, though, struggled to arrange the issue to his liking, complaining in a letter of 1st December 1854 to Mrs Richard Watson that he was 'so much disappointed in the nature of the Contributions as yet received, that it will require my utmost care and assistance'. He reserved a week to work on finishing *The Seven Poor Travellers*, explaining that he would certainly be occupied for the entire day on Friday 8th December because on Saturday, the number 'must be upon the Steam Engine, printing'. We do not know which stories Dickens had received as of the 1st, nor his precise complaints about them, but his letter provides a glimpse into his thought process. Fretting over the Christmas issue right up until the final moment, casting himself as something of a victim of his contributors despite his own usually vague directions to them, Dickens was committed to holiday storytelling success even if it created unwelcome additional stress.

Early in this number, the first traveller makes his case to the matron of the almshouse by reminding her that 'Christmas comes but once a year – which is unhappily too true, for when it begins to stay with us the whole year round, we shall make this earth a very different place.' His plea echoes Ebenezer Scrooge's declaration at the close of his visit with the Spirit of Christmas Future: 'I will honour Christmas in my heart, and try to keep it all the year.' *A Christmas Carol* (1843) was eleven years old by the time Dickens was composing *The Seven Poor Travellers*, but it remained popular with Victorian audiences. By gesturing towards its moral message so early in this Christmas issue, Dickens signalled a return of the themes that audiences knew they liked. Those themes were not always as cheerily pleasant as modern-day renditions of Victorian Christmas tales suggest; as *Carol* features a frightening depiction of Ignorance and Want in the form of animalistic starved children, the stories in the Christmas numbers regularly feature ghosts (some not as benevolent as the ones Scrooge encounters), murder, betrayal and suffering with peace and redemption sometime absent.

The stories in this collection are no exception. Sala's account of Acon-Virlaz and Ben-Daoud disturbingly relies upon unoriginal anti-Semitic stereotypes, and anti-Semitism resurfaces briefly in Collins' story. Sala's Acon-Virlaz is a forumulaic caricature of a Jew obsessed with wealth, weighed down by gold and jewels he cannot resist, and although women and children from all over the world block the way to the exit in his dream, those figures are not described with the disgust the narrator reserves for Acon-Virlaz and Ben-Daoud's features. Dickens, who had faced criticism for his rendering of Fagin in *Oliver Twist* (1837–39), clearly did not feel that Sala's offensive descriptions needed changing. Eliza Lynn Linton's story of the sixth poor traveller powerfully introduces ghosts to the number. Mary is first visited by her dead sister Ellen and then haunted by a living man, her husband, as she suffers from constant fear of his pursuit and his violence. Her wearing of widow's weeds does nothing to dispel from the story the creepy lingering presence of an uncaptured murderer who could walk through the door of Watts' Charity at any moment.

Wilkie Collins, the only writer who had not written for a Christmas number before, sent a remarkable contribution. The fourth traveller's story has the distinction of being regarded as the first published British detective story. Later reprinted as 'The Lawyer's Story of A Stolen Letter' in Collins' 1856 collection *After Dark*, the tale is similar to Edgar Allen Poe's 'The Purloined Letter' (1845), and Poe's stories were important influences as Collins developed longer mystery narratives. The story of the fourth traveller also plays delightfully with the whole notion of what a story is. For a storyteller to declare, 'Now, I absolutely decline to tell you a story,' in order to insist on the tale's definition as a 'statement' not only anticipates detective novels in which documents become narrators but also teases readers and perhaps reveals a bit of Collins teasing his friend Dickens, the powerful editor in chief. With its account of the hiccupping tart-filled boy and its rebuffs of the 'man in the corner' who wants to identify people in the story (especially the tantalisingly described governess with 'kiss-and-come-again sort of lips'), the humour of Collins' piece meshes well with the other stories.

Light-hearted moments consistently relieve the seriousness of these tales. Bizarre 'live armadillos with their jewelled scales' distract from Acon-Virlaz offering up his daughter as a piece of property as he tries to retain his treasure. An elderly looking, curious eight-year-old tenderly touches the fifth traveller's coat to experience its texture then insists that the man display his tongue because it must be the source of such a foreign-sounding accent. And in Dickens' own set-up story, humour and serious comment are woven together seamlessly.

Prior to meeting 'his travellers', the narrator somewhat sadistically enjoys imagining more and more destitution for them so that he can delight all the more in alleviating their suffering: 'I made them footsore; I made them weary; I made them carry packs and bundles; I made them stop by finger-posts and milestones, leaning on their bent sticks and looking wistfully at what was written there; I made them lose their way, and filled their five wits with apprehensions of lying out all night, and being frozen to death.' As self-serving as it is altruistic, this model of charity illustrates the disturbing quality of some philanthropic mindsets. Without vilifying the traveller – indeed the narrator's tone remains humourous – the story gently opens one's eyes to the problem of self-interested giving. The parading of the donated feast down the High Street is at once inspiring and ridiculous, complete with a boy sprinting down the road with hot desserts at the cue of a whistle.

Ultimately, Dickens was pleased with at least a majority of *The Seven Poor Travellers*, as were his readers. Ironically,

Dickens also briefly shared his readers' ignorance of who wrote each story. Dickens admired Procter's poem but was unaware that she was its author until the number was already at press. Procter had been sending her submissions to *Household Words* under the pseudonym of Mary Berwick, and Dickens did not find out that Procter was Berwick until after he had unknowingly praised her poem for this number in her presence. When his sub-editor W.H. Wills revealed her identity, he wrote to Procter to dispel his embarrassment, complimenting her talent while also reasserting his authority as he called himself Richard Watts and bestowed 'blessing and forgiveness' upon her (17th December 1854). In a letter of 3rd January 1855, Dickens noted that 80,000 copies of this number had already been sold, and he took credit for those sales himself, citing the strength of 'the first ten pages or so', which contained his story of Richard Doubledick. Multiple stage adaptations also attest to the number's popularity, and, although Dickens' story of Doubledick features heavily in them, so do the other stories and Procter's poem, suggesting that Dickens' 'ten pages or so' were not solely responsible for the collection's success.

Most adaptations seized upon the melodramatic potential of the story of Richard Doubledick and Captain Taunton. With the Crimean War in progress, the dedication of a soldier during the Napolenoic Wars was also a timely topic. The bond between Taunton and Doubledick is so immediately strong that simply being in Taunton's presence shames Doubledick so intensely that he breaks down crying and kisses Taunton's hand. The story emphasises the gaze of Taunton's dark bright eyes and, through Taunton's declaration that a man who could cry such tears could not bear 'such marks' of flogging, suggests that Taunton is physically familiar with Doubledick in addition to holding knowledge about what Doubledick's soul can and cannot bear. Coupling a touching tenderness with an intense male bond that leads to a battlefield partnership of thirteen years, the story of Doubledick and Taunton guaranteed the success of dramatisations, but the staged versions also interwove the other travellers' stories. Procter's poem becomes much more violent in some scripts while others rename characters to create the illusion of distance from Dickens' collection, calling the sisters from Lynn Linton's story, for instance, 'Oak' and 'Willow'.

Following the standard protocol for *Household Words*, Dickens' name was the only one that appeared in print on this number, which stated that it was 'Conducted by Charles Dickens'. The practice of naming only Dickens led to many of the pieces being misattributed to him. In the United States, *Harper's New Monthly Magazine* reprinted Collins' and Lynn Linton's stories with Dickens as the named author in February of 1855, and Sala's writings for *Household Words* have often been mistaken for Dickens' own. In many ways, however, the different voices of these travellers are as distinct as the experiences they relate. That those voices are shared in this number without jarring shifts is a testament to its quality.

As *The Seven Poor Travellers* draws to a close, the poignant picture of mists surrounding the narrator as he departs from Kent anticipates one of the dominant images from *Great Expectations*, which Dickens would publish six years after this Christmas number. The idea that a solitary person may connect with others at the Christmas season to pass time pleasantly by sharing food and stories parallels what readers past as well as present might do as they purchase this special

Christmas issue – share the tales with their own companions, whether they be kin or fellow lonely travellers.

– Melisa Klimaszewski, 2010

NOTE ON THE TEXT

The Seven Poor Travellers was originally published in December of 1854 as a special issue or number of *Household Words*, the weekly journal that Charles Dickens founded in 1850 and for which he served as chief editor. The original publication did not identify the contributor of each story, stating only that the number was 'Conducted by Charles Dickens'. This edition identifies the author of each story.

In February of 1855 the American *Harper's New Monthly Magazine* reprinted several of the tales in this number under Dickens' name. Wilkie Collins' 'The Fourth Poor Traveller' appeared as 'A Lawyer's Story' and Eliza Lynn Linton's 'The Sixth Poor Traveller' appeared as 'The Widow's Story'. Collins later published his contribution as 'The Lawyer's Story of A Stolen Letter' in his collection *After Dark* (1856), which also uses a linking frame concept. Dickens' own story of Richard Doubledick appeared as 'The Redeemed Profligate' and followed an instalment of William M. Thackeray's novel, *The Newcomes*.

My editorial practices preserve the text's original punctuation and capitalisation with a minimum of modernisation. I have retained inconsistent capitalisation because Dickens and his colleagues so often used capitalisation for emphasis or for other intentional reasons. Except in cases of obvious printer errors (such as 'placs' for 'places') or instances where an apparent punctuation error obscures meaning, I have retained the text's original punctuation, which includes more commas than might be used today and semicolons where today's practices would call for commas.

The most standardisation appears in regard to hyphens. I have modernised hyphenated words (such as to-morrow and up-stairs) that are now understood as single words, and I follow Oxford's guidelines regarding compound words that take hyphens when attributive.

These practices are consistent with other collaborative Dickens works, such as his annual Christmas numbers, now in print from Hesperus.

The Seven Poor Travellers

Being the Extra Christmas Number
Of Household Words

Conducted By Charles Dickens

Containing The Amount Of
One Number And A Half

Christmas, 1854

THE FIRST
[by Charles Dickens]

Strictly speaking, there were only six Poor Travellers; but, being a Traveller myself, though an idle one, and being withal as poor as I hope to be, I brought the number up to seven. This word of explanation is due at once, for what says the inscription over the quaint old door?

RICHARD WATTS, Esq.
by his Will, dated 22 Aug. 1579,
founded this Charity
for Six poor Travellers,
who not being ROGUES, or PROCTORS,
May receive gratis for one Night,
Lodging, Entertainment,
and Four-pence each.

It was in the ancient little city of Rochester in Kent, of all the good days in the year upon a Christmas Eve, that I stood reading this inscription over the quaint old door in question. I had been wandering about the neighbouring Cathedral, and had seen the tomb of Richard Watts,[1] with the effigy of worthy Master Richard starting out of it like a ship's figure-head; and I had felt that I could do no less, as I gave the Verger[2] his fee, than inquire the way to Watts's Charity. The way being very short and very plain, I had come prosperously to the inscription and the quaint old door.

'Now,' said I to myself, as I looked at the knocker, 'I know I am not a Proctor;[3] I wonder whether I am a Rogue!'

Upon the whole, though Conscience reproduced two or three pretty faces which might have had smaller attraction for a moral Goliath than they had had for me, who am but a Tom Thumb in that way, I came to the conclusion that I was not a Rogue. So, beginning to regard the establishment as in some sort my property, bequeathed to me and divers co-legatees, share and share alike, by the Worshipful Master Richard Watts, I stepped backward into the road to survey my inheritance.

I found it to be a clean white house, of a staid and venerable air, with the quaint old door already three times mentioned (an arched door), choice little long low lattice-windows, and a roof of three gables. The silent High Street of Rochester is full of gables, with old beams and timbers carved into strange faces. It is oddly garnished with a queer old clock that projects over the pavement out of a grave red brick building, as if Time carried on business there, and hung out his sign. Sooth to say, he did an active stroke of work in Rochester, in the old days of the Romans, and the Saxons, and the Normans, and down to the times of King John,[4] when the rugged castle – I will not undertake to say how many hundreds of years old then – was abandoned to the centuries of weather which have so defaced the dark apertures in its walls, that the ruin looks as if the rooks and daws had picked its eyes out.

I was very well pleased, both with my property and its situation. While I was yet surveying it with growing content, I espied at one of the upper lattices which stood open, a decent body, of a wholesome matronly appearance, whose eyes I caught inquiringly addressed to mine. They said so plainly, 'Do you wish to see the house?' that I answered aloud, 'Yes, if you please.' And within a minute the old door opened, and I bent my head, and went down two steps into the entry.

'This,' said the matronly presence, ushering me into a low room on the right, 'is where the Travellers sit by the fire, and cook what bits of suppers they buy with their fourpences.'

'Oh! Then they have no Entertainment?' said I. For, the inscription over the outer door was still running in my head, and I was mentally repeating in a kind of tune, 'Lodging, entertainment, and fourpence each.'

'They have a fire provided for 'em,' returned the matron: a mighty civil person, not, as I could make out, overpaid: 'and these cooking utensils. And this what's painted on a board, is the rules for their behaviour. They have their fourpences when they get their tickets from the steward over the way – for I don't admit 'em myself, they must get their tickets first – and sometimes one buys a rasher of bacon, and another a herring, and another a pound of potatoes, or what not. Sometimes, two or three of 'em will club their fourpences together, and make a supper that way. But, not much of anything is to be got for fourpence, at present, when provisions is so dear.'

'True indeed,' I remarked. I had been looking about the room, admiring its snug fireside at the upper end, its glimpse of the street through the low mullioned window,[5] and its beams overhead. 'It is very comfortable,' said I.

'Ill-convenient,' observed the matronly presence.

I liked to hear her say so; for, it showed a commendable anxiety to execute in no niggardly spirit the intentions of Master Richard Watts. But, the room was really so well adapted to its purpose that I protested, quite enthusiastically, against her disparagement.

'Nay, ma'am,' said I, 'I am sure it is warm in winter and cool in summer. It has a look of homely welcome and soothing rest. It has a remarkably cosey fireside, the very blink of which, gleaming out into the street upon a winter night, is enough to warm all Rochester's heart. And as to the convenience of the six Poor Travellers –'

'I don't mean them,' returned the presence. 'I speak of its being an ill-conwenience to myself and my daughter having no other room to sit in of a night.'

This was true enough, but there was another quaint room of corresponding dimensions on the opposite side of the entry: so, I stepped across to it, through the open doors of both rooms, and asked what this chamber was for?

'This,' returned the presence, 'is the Board Room. Where the gentlemen meet when they come here.'

Let me see. I had counted from the street six upper windows besides these on the ground story. Making a per-plexed calculation in my mind, I rejoined, 'Then the six Poor Travellers sleep upstairs?'

My new friend shook her head. 'They sleep,' she an-swered, 'in two little outer galleries at the back, where their beds has always been, ever since the Charity was founded. It being so very ill-conwenient to me as things is at present, the gentlemen are going to take off a bit of the back yard and make a slip of a room for 'em there, to sit in before they go to bed.'

'And then the six Poor Travellers,' said I, 'will be entirely out of the house?'

'Entirely out of the house,' assented the presence, com-fortably smoothing her hands. 'Which is considered much better for all parties, and much more conwenient.'

I had been a little startled, in the cathedral, by the emphasis with which the effigy of Master Richard Watts was bursting out of his tomb; but, I began to think, now, that it might be expected to come across the High Street some stormy night, and make a disturbance here.

Howbeit, I kept my thoughts to myself, and accompanied the presence to the little galleries at the back. I found them, on a tiny scale, like the galleries in old inn-yards; and they were very clean. While I was looking at them, the matron gave me to understand that the prescribed number of Poor Travellers were forthcoming every night from year's end to year's end; and that the beds were always occupied. My questions upon this, and her replies, brought us back to the Board Room so essential to the dignity of 'the gentlemen,' where she showed me the printed accounts of the Charity hanging up by the window. From them, I gathered that the greater part of the property bequeathed by the Worshipful Master Richard Watts for the maintenance of this foundation, was, at the period of his death, mere marshland; but that, in course of time, it had been reclaimed and built upon, and was very considerably increased in value. I found, too, that about a thirtieth part of the annual revenue was now expended on the purposes commemorated in the inscription over the door: the rest being handsomely laid out in Chancery,[6] law expenses, collectorship, receivership, poundage, and other appendages of management, highly complimentary to the importance of the six Poor Travellers. In short, I made the not entirely new discovery that it may be said of an establishment like this, in dear Old England, as of the fat oyster in the American story, that it takes a good many men to swallow it whole.[7]

'And pray, ma'am,' said I, sensible that the blankness of my face began to brighten as a thought occurred to me, 'could one see these Travellers?'

Well! she returned dubiously; no! 'Not tonight, for instance?' said I. Well! she returned more positively; no. Nobody ever asked to see them, and nobody ever did see them.

As I am not easily baulked in a design when I am set upon it, I urged to the good lady that this was Christmas Eve; that Christmas comes but once a year – which is unhappily too true, for when it begins to stay with us the whole year round, we shall make this earth a very different place; that I was possessed by the desire to treat the Travellers to a supper and a temperate glass of hot Wassail; that the voice of Fame had been heard in the land, declaring my ability to make hot Wassail;[8] that if I were permitted to hold the feast, I should be found conformable to reason, sobriety, and good hours; in a word, that I could be merry and wise myself, and had been even known at a pinch to keep others so, although I was decorated with no badge or medal, and was not a Brother, Orator, Apostle, Saint, or Prophet of any denomination whatever. In the end, I prevailed, to my great joy. It was settled that at nine o'clock that night, a Turkey and a piece of Roast Beef should smoke upon the board; and that I, faint and unworthy minister for once of Master Richard Watts, should preside as the Christmas supper host of the six Poor Travellers.

I went back to my inn, to give the necessary directions for the Turkey and Roast Beef, and, during the remainder of the day, could settle to nothing for thinking of the Poor Travellers. When the wind blew hard against the windows – it was a cold day, with dark gusts of sleet alternating with periods of wild brightness, as if the year were dying fitfully – I pictured them advancing towards their resting place along various cold roads, and felt delighted to think how little they foresaw the supper that awaited them. I painted their portraits in my mind, and indulged in little heightening touches. I made them footsore; I made them weary; I made them carry packs and bundles; I made them stop by fingerposts and milestones, leaning on their bent sticks and looking wistfully at what was written there; I made them lose their way, and filled their five wits with apprehensions of lying out all night, and being frozen to death. I took up my hat and went out, climbed to the top of the Old Castle, and looked over the windy hills that slope down to the Medway: almost believing that I could descry some of my Travellers in the distance. After it fell dark, and the Cathedral bell was heard in the invisible steeple – quite a bower of frosty rime[9] when I had last seen it – striking five, six, seven; I became so full of my Travellers that I could eat no dinner, and felt constrained to watch them still, in the red coals of my fire. They were all arrived by this time, I thought, had got their tickets, and were gone in. – There, my pleasure was dashed by the reflection that probably some Travellers had come too late and were shut out.

After the Cathedral bell had struck eight, I could smell a delicious savour of Turkey and Roast Beef rising to the window of my adjoining bedroom, which looked down into the inn-yard, just where the lights of the kitchen reddened a massive fragment of the Castle Wall. It was high time to make the Wassail now; therefore, I had up the materials (which, together with their proportions and combinations, I must decline to impart, as the only secret of my own I was ever known to keep), and made a glorious jorum.[10] Not in a bowl; for, a bowl anywhere but on a shelf, is a low superstition fraught with cooling and slopping; but, in a brown earthenware pitcher, tenderly suffocated when full, with a coarse cloth. It being now upon the stroke of nine, I set out for Watts's Charity, carrying my brown beauty in my arms. I would trust Ben the waiter with untold gold; but, there are strings in the human heart which must never be sounded by another, and drinks that I make myself are those strings in mine.

The Travellers were all assembled, the cloth was laid, and Ben had brought a great billet of wood, and had laid it artfully on the top of the fire, so that a touch or two of the poker after supper should make a roaring blaze. Having deposited my brown beauty in a red nook of the hearth inside the fender, where she soon began to sing like an ethereal cricket, diffusing at the same time odours as of ripe vineyards, spice forests, and orange groves – I say, having stationed my beauty in a place of security and improvement, I introduced myself to my guests by shaking hands all round, and giving them a hearty welcome.

I found the party to be thus composed. Firstly, myself. Secondly, a very decent man indeed, with his right arm in a sling; who had a certain clean, agreeable smell of wood about him, from which I judged him to have something to do with shipbuilding. Thirdly, a little sailor-boy, a mere child, with a profusion of rich dark brown hair, and deep womanly-looking eyes. Fourthly, a shabby-genteel personage in a threadbare black suit, and apparently in very bad circumstances, with a dry suspicious look; the absent buttons on his waistcoat eked out with red tape; and a bundle of extraordinarily tattered papers sticking out of an inner breast pocket. Fifthly, a foreigner by birth, but an Englishman in speech, who carried his pipe in the band of his hat, and lost no time in telling me, in an easy, simple, engaging way, that he was a watchmaker from Geneva, and travelled all about the continent, mostly on foot, working as a journeyman, and seeing new countries – possibly (I thought) also smuggling a watch or so, now and then. Sixthly, a little widow, who had been very pretty and was still very young, but whose beauty had been wrecked in some great misfortune, and whose manner was remarkably timid, scared, and solitary. Seventhly and lastly, a Traveller of a kind familiar to my boyhood, but now almost obsolete: a Book Pedlar: who had a quantity of Pamphlets and Numbers with him, and who presently boasted that he could repeat more verses in an evening, than he could sell in a twelvemonth.

All these I have mentioned, in the order in which they sat at table. I presided, and the matronly presence faced me. We were not long in taking our places, for the supper had arrived with me, in the following procession.

Myself with the pitcher.

Ben with Beer.

Inattentive Boy with hot plates.|Inattentive Boy with hot plates.

THE TURKEY.

Female carrying sauces to be heated on the spot.

THE BEEF.

Man with Tray on his head, containing

Vegetables and Sundries.

Volunteer hostler[11] from Hotel, grinning,

And rendering no assistance.

As we passed along the High Street, Comet-like, we left a long tail of fragrance behind us which caused the public to stop, sniffing in wonder. We had previously left at the corner of the inn-yard, a wall-eyed young man connected with the Fly department,[12] and well accustomed to the sound of a railway whistle which Ben always carries in his pocket: whose instructions were, so soon as he should hear the whistle blown, to dash into the kitchen, seize the hot plum pudding and mince pies, and speed with them to Watts's Charity: where they would be received (he was further instructed) by the sauce-female, who would be provided with brandy in a blue state of combustion.

All these arrangements were executed in the most exact and punctual manner. I never saw a finer turkey, finer beef, or greater prodigality of sauce and gravy; and my Travellers did wonderful justice to everything set before them. It made my heart rejoice, to observe how their wind-and-frost-hardened faces, softened in the clatter of plates and knives and forks, and mellowed in the fire and supper heat. While their hats and caps, and wrappers, hanging up; a few small bundles on the ground in a corner; and, in another corner, three or four old walking sticks, worn down at the end to mere fringe; linked this snug interior with the bleak outside in a golden chain.

When supper was done, and my brown beauty had been elevated on the table, there was a general requisition to me, to 'take the corner;' which suggested to me, comfortably enough, how much my friends here made of a fire – for when had *I* ever thought so highly of the corner, since the days when I connected it with Jack Horner?[13] However, as I declined, Ben, whose touch on all convivial instruments is perfect, drew the table apart, and instructing my Travellers to open right and left on either side of me, and form round the fire, closed up the centre with myself and my chair, and preserved the order we had kept at table. He had already, in a tranquil manner, boxed the ears of the inattentive boys until they had been by imperceptible degrees boxed out of the room; and he now rapidly skirmished the sauce-female into the High Street, disappeared, and softly closed the door.

This was the time for bringing the poker to bear on the billet of wood. I tapped it three times, like an enchanted talisman, and a brilliant host of merrymakers burst out of it, and sported off by the chimney – rushing up the middle in a fiery country dance, and never coming down again. Meanwhile, by their sparkling light which threw our lamp into the shade,

I filled the glasses, and gave my Travellers, CHRISTMAS! – CHRISTMAS EVE, my friends, when the Shepherds, who were Poor Travellers too in their way, heard the Angels sing, 'On earth, peace. Goodwill towards men!'[14]

I don't know who was the first among us to think that we ought to take hands as we sat, in deference to the toast, or whether any one of us anticipated the others, but at any rate we all did it. We then drank to the memory of the good Master Richard Watts. And I wish his Ghost may never have had worse usage under that roof, than it had from us!

It was the witching time for Storytelling. 'Our whole life, Travellers,' said I, 'is a story more or less intelligible – generally less; but, we shall read it by a clearer light when it is ended. I for one, am so divided this night between fact and fiction, that I scarce know which is which. Shall we beguile the time by telling stories, in our order as we sit here?'

They all answered, Yes, provided I would begin. I had little to tell them, but I was bound by my own proposal. Therefore, after looking for a while at the spiral column of smoke wreathing up from my brown beauty, through which I could have almost sworn I saw the effigy of Master Richard Watts less startled than usual; I fired away.

In the year one thousand seven hundred and ninety-nine, a relative of mine came limping down, on foot, to this town of Chatham. I call it this town, because if anybody present knows to a nicety where Rochester ends and Chatham begins, it is more than I do. He was a poor traveller, with not a farthing in his pocket. He sat by the fire in this very room, and he slept one night in a bed that will be occupied tonight by someone here.

My relative came down to Chatham, to enlist in a cavalry regiment, if a cavalry regiment would have him; if not, to take

King George's shilling from any corporal or sergeant who would put a bunch of ribbons in his hat.[15] His object was, to get shot; but, he thought he might as well ride to death as be at the trouble of walking.

My relative's Christian name was Richard, but he was better known as Dick. He dropped his own surname on the road down, and took up that of Doubledick. He was passed as Richard Doubledick; age twenty-two; height, five foot ten; native place, Exmouth; which he had never been near in his life. There was no cavalry in Chatham when he limped over the bridge here with half a shoe to his dusty foot, so he enlisted into a regiment of the line, and was glad to get drunk and forget all about it.

You are to know that this relative of mine had gone wrong and run wild. His heart was in the right place, but it was sealed up. He had been betrothed to a good and beautiful girl whom he had loved better than she – or perhaps even he – believed; but, in an evil hour, he had given her cause to say to him, solemnly, 'Richard, I will never marry any other man. I will live single for your sake, but Mary Marshall's lips;' her name was Mary Marshall; 'never address another word to you on earth. Go, Richard! Heaven forgive you!' This finished him. This brought him down to Chatham. This made him Private Richard Doubledick, with a determination to be shot.

There was not a more dissipated and reckless soldier in Chatham barracks, in the year one thousand seven hundred and ninety-nine, than Private Richard Doubledick. He associated with the dregs of every regiment, he was as seldom sober as he could be, and was constantly under punishment. It became clear to the whole barracks, that Private Richard Doubledick would very soon be flogged.

Now, the Captain of Richard Doubledick's company was a young gentleman not above five years his senior, whose eyes had an expression in them which affected Private Richard Doubledick in a very remarkable way. They were bright, handsome, dark eyes – what are called laughing eyes generally, and, when serious, rather steady than severe – but, they were the only eyes now left in his narrowed world that Private Richard Doubledick could not stand. Unabashed by evil report and punishment, defiant of everything else and everybody else, he had but to know that those eyes looked at him for a moment, and he felt ashamed. He could not so much as salute Captain Taunton in the street, like any other officer. He was reproached and confused – troubled by the mere possibility of the captain's looking at him. In his worst moments he would rather turn back and go any distance out of his way, than encounter those two handsome, dark, bright eyes.

One day, when Private Richard Doubledick came out of the Black hole,[16] where he had been passing the last eight-and-forty hours, and in which retreat he spent a good deal of his time, he was ordered to betake himself to Captain Taunton's quarters. In the stale and squalid state of a man just out of the Black hole, he had less fancy than ever for being seen by the captain; but, he was not so mad yet as to disobey orders, and consequently went up to the terrace overlooking the parade ground, where the officers' quarters were: twisting and breaking in his hands as he went along, a bit of the straw that had formed the decorative furniture of the Black hole.

'Come in!' cried the Captain, when he knocked with his knuckles at the door. Private Richard Doubledick pulled off his cap, took a stride forward, and felt very conscious that he stood in the light of the dark bright eyes.

There was a silent pause. Private Richard Doubledick had put the straw in his mouth, and was gradually doubling it up into his windpipe and choking himself.

'Doubledick,' said the Captain, 'Do you know where you are going to?'

'To the Devil, sir?' faltered Doubledick.

'Yes,' returned the Captain. 'And very fast.'

Private Richard Doubledick turned the straw of the Black hole in his mouth, and made a miserable salute of acquiescence.

'Doubledick,' said the Captain, 'since I entered his Majesty's service, a boy of seventeen, I have been pained to see many men of promise going that road; but, I have never been so pained to see a man determined to make the shameful journey, as I have been, ever since you joined the regiment, to see you.'

Private Richard Doubledick began to find a film stealing over the floor at which he looked; also to find the legs of the Captain's breakfast table turning crooked, as if he saw them through water.

'I am only a common soldier, sir,' said he. 'It signifies very little what such a poor brute comes to.'

'You are a man,' returned the Captain with grave indignation, 'of education and superior advantages; and if you say that, meaning what you say, you have sunk lower than I had believed. How low that must be, I leave you to consider: knowing what I know of your disgrace, and seeing what I see.'

'I hope to get shot soon, sir,' said Private Richard Doubledick; 'and then the regiment, and the world together, will be rid of me.'

The legs of the table were becoming very crooked. Doubledick, looking up to steady his vision, met the eyes that had so strong an influence over him. He put his hand before his own eyes, and the breast of his disgrace-jacket[17] swelled as if it would fly asunder.

'I would rather,' said the young Captain, 'see this in you, Doubledick, than I would see five thousand guineas counted out upon this table for a gift to my good mother. Have you a mother?'

'I am thankful to say she is dead, sir.'

'If your praises,' returned the Captain, 'were sounded from mouth to mouth through the whole regiment, through the whole army, through the whole country, you would wish she had lived, to say with pride and joy, "He is my son!"'

'Spare me, sir;' said Doubledick. 'She would never have heard any good of me. She would never have had any pride and joy in owning herself my mother. Love and compassion she might have had, and would have always had, I know; but not – Spare me, sir! I am a broken wretch, quite at your mercy!' And he turned his face to the wall, and stretched out his imploring hand.

'My friend – ' began the captain.

'God bless you, sir!' sobbed Private Richard Doubledick.

'You are at the crisis of your fate. Hold your course unchanged, a little longer, and you know what must happen. *I* know even better than you can imagine, that after that has happened, you are lost. No man who could shed those tears, could bear those marks.'[18]

'I fully believe it, sir,' in a low, shivering voice, said Private Richard Doubledick.

'But a man in any station can do his duty,' said the young Captain, 'and, in doing it, can earn his own respect, even if his case should be so very unfortunate and so very rare, that he can earn no other man's. A common soldier, poor brute though you called him just now, has this advantage in the stormy times we live in, that he always does his duty before a host of sympathising witnesses. Do you doubt that he may so do it as to be extolled through a whole regiment, through a whole army, through a whole country? Turn while you may yet retrieve the past, and try.'

'I will! I ask for only one witness, sir,' cried Richard, with a bursting heart.

'I understand you. I will be a watchful and a faithful one.'

I have heard from Private Richard Doubledick's own lips, that he dropped down upon his knee, kissed that officer's hand, arose, and went out of the light of the dark bright eyes, an altered man.

In that year, one thousand seven hundred and ninety-nine, the French were in Egypt, in Italy, in Germany, where not? Napoleon Buonaparte had likewise begun to stir against us in India, and most men could read the signs of the great troubles that were coming on. In the very next year, when we formed an alliance with Austria against him, Captain Taunton's regiment was on service in India. And there was not a finer non-commissioned officer in it – no, nor in the whole line – than Corporal Richard Doubledick.

In eighteen hundred and one, the Indian army were on the coast of Egypt. Next year was the year of the proclamation of the short peace, and they were recalled. It had then become well known to thousands of men, that wherever Captain Taunton with the dark bright eyes, led, there, close to him, ever at his side, firm as a rock, true as the sun, and brave as Mars,[19] would be certain to be found, while life beat in their hearts, that famous soldier, Sergeant Richard Doubledick.

Eighteen hundred and five, besides being the great year of Trafalgar,[20] was a year of hard fighting in India. That year saw such wonders done by a Sergeant-Major, who cut his way single-handed through a solid mass of men, recovered the colours of his regiment which had been seized from the hand of a poor boy shot through the heart, and rescued his wounded captain, who was down, and in a very jungle of horses' hoofs and sabres – saw such wonders done, I say, by this brave Sergeant-Major, that he was specially made the bearer of the colours he had won; and Ensign Richard Doubledick had risen from the ranks.

Sorely cut up in every battle, but always reinforced by the bravest of men – for, the fame of following the old colours, shot through and through, which Ensign Richard Doubledick had saved, inspired all breasts – this regiment fought its way through the Peninsular war, up to the investment of Badajos in eighteen hundred and twelve.[21] Again and again it had been cheered through the British ranks until the tears had sprung into men's eyes at the mere hearing of the mighty British voice so exultant in their valour; and there was not a drummer-boy but knew the legend, that wherever the two friends, Major Taunton with the dark bright eyes, and Ensign Richard Doubledick who was devoted to him, were seen to go, there the boldest spirits in the English army became wild to follow.

One day, at Badajos – not in the great storming, but in repelling a hot sally of the besieged upon our men at work in the trenches, who had given way, the two officers found themselves hurrying forward, face to face, against a party of French infantry who made a stand. There was an officer at their head, encouraging his men – a courageous, handsome, gallant officer of five and thirty – whom Doubledick saw hurriedly, almost momentarily, but saw well. He particularly noticed this officer waving his sword, and rallying his men with an eager and excited cry, when they fired in obedience to his gesture, and Major Taunton dropped.

It was over in ten minutes more, and Doubledick returned to the spot where he had laid the best friend man ever had, on a coat spread upon the wet clay. Major Taunton's uniform was opened at the breast, and on his shirt were three little spots of blood.

'Dear Doubledick,' said he, 'I am dying.'

'For the love of Heaven, no!' exclaimed the other, kneeling down beside him, and passing his arm round his neck to raise his head. 'Taunton! My preserver, my guardian angel, my witness! Dearest, truest, kindest of human beings! Taunton! For God's sake!'

The bright dark eyes – so very, very dark now, in the pale face – smiled upon him; and the hand he had kissed thirteen years ago, laid itself fondly on his breast.

'Write to my mother. You will see Home again. Tell her how we became friends. It will comfort her, as it comforts me.'

He spoke no more, but faintly signed for a moment towards his hair as it fluttered in the wind. The Ensign understood him. He smiled again when he saw that, and gently turning his face over on the supporting arm as if for rest, died, with his hand upon the breast in which he had revived a soul.

No dry eye looked on Ensign Richard Doubledick, that melancholy day. He buried his friend on the field, and became a lone, bereaved man. Beyond his duty he appeared to have but two remaining cares in life; one, to preserve the little packet of hair he was to give to Taunton's mother; the other, to encounter that French officer who had rallied the men under whose fire Taunton fell. A new legend now began to circulate among our troops; and it was, that when he and the French officer came face to face once more, there would be weeping in France.

The war went on – and through it went the exact picture of the French officer on the one side, and the bodily reality upon the other – until the Battle of Toulouse was fought.[22] In the returns sent home, appeared these words: 'Severely wounded, but not dangerously, Lieutenant Richard Doubledick.'

At Midsummer time in the year eighteen hundred and fourteen, Lieutenant Richard Doubledick, now a browned soldier, seven and thirty years of age, came home to England, invalided. He brought the hair with him, near his heart. Many a French officer had he seen, since that day; many a dreadful night, in searching with men and lanterns for his wounded, had he relieved French officers lying disabled; but, the mental picture and the reality had never come together.

Though he was weak and suffered pain, he lost not an hour in getting down to Frome in Somersetshire, where Taunton's mother lived. In the sweet, compassionate words that naturally present themselves to the mind tonight, 'he was the only son of his mother, and she was a widow.'[23]

It was a Sunday evening, and the lady sat at her quiet garden window, reading the Bible; reading to herself, in a trembling voice, that very passage in it as I have heard him tell. He heard the words; 'Young man, I say unto thee, arise!'[24]

He had to pass the window; and the bright dark eyes of his debased time seemed to look at him. Her heart told her who he was; she came to the door, quickly, and fell upon his neck.

'He saved me from ruin, made me a human creature, won me from infamy and shame. O God, forever bless him! As He will, He will!'

'He will!' the lady answered. 'I know he is in Heaven!' Then she piteously cried, 'But, O, my darling boy, my darling boy!'

Never, from the hour when Private Richard Doubledick enlisted at Chatham, had the Private, Corporal, Sergeant,

Sergeant-Major, Ensign, or Lieutenant, breathed his right name, or the name of Mary Marshall, or a word of the story of his life, into any ear, except his reclaimer's. That previous scene in his existence was closed. He had firmly resolved that his expiation should be, to live unknown; to disturb no more the peace that had long grown over his old offences; to let it be revealed when he was dead, that he had striven and suffered, and had never forgotten; and then, if they could forgive him and believe him – well, it would be time enough – time enough!

But, that night, remembering the words he had cherished for two years, 'Tell her how we became friends. It will comfort her, as it comforts me,' he related everything. It gradually seemed to him, as if in his maturity he had recovered a mother; it gradually seemed to her, as if in her bereavement she had found a son. During his stay in England, the quiet garden into which he had slowly and painfully crept, a stranger, became the boundary of his home; when he was able to rejoin his regiment in the spring, he left the garden, thinking was this indeed the first time he had ever turned his face towards the old colours, with a woman's blessing!

He followed them – so ragged, so scarred and pierced now, that they would scarcely hold together – to Quatre Bras, and Ligny.[25] He stood beside them, in an awful stillness of many men, shadowy through the mist and drizzle of a wet June forenoon, on the field of Waterloo. And down to that hour, the picture in his mind of the French officer had never been compared with the reality.

The famous regiment was in action early in the battle, and received its first check in many an eventful year, when he was seen to fall. But, it swept on to avenge him, and left behind it no such creature in the world of consciousness, as Lieutenant Richard Doubledick.

Through pits of mire, and pools of rain; along deep ditches, once roads, that were pounded and ploughed to pieces by artillery, heavy waggons, tramp of men and horses, and the struggle of every wheeled thing that could carry wounded soldiers; jolted among the dying and the dead, so disfigured by blood and mud as to be hardly recognisable for humanity; undisturbed by the moaning of men and the shrieking of horses, which, newly taken from the peaceful pursuits of life, could not endure the sight of the stragglers lying by the wayside, never to resume their toilsome journey; dead, as to any sentient life that was in it, and yet alive; the form that had been Lieutenant Richard Doubledick, with whose praises England rang, was conveyed to Brussels. There, it was tenderly laid down in hospital: and there it lay, week after week, through the long bright summer days, until the harvest, spared by war, had ripened and was gathered in.

Over and over again, the sun rose and set upon the crowded city; over and over again, the moonlight nights were quiet on the plains of Waterloo; and all that time was a blank to what had been Lieutenant Richard Doubledick. Rejoicing troops marched into Brussels, and marched out; brothers and fathers, sisters, mothers, and wives, came thronging thither, drew their lots of joy or agony, and departed; so many times a day, the bells rang; so many times, the shadows of the great buildings changed; so many lights sprang up at dusk; so many feet passed here and there upon the pavements; so many hours of sleep and cooler air of night succeeded; indifferent to all, a marble face lay on a bed, like the face of a recumbent statue on the tomb of Lieutenant Richard Doubledick.

Slowly labouring, at last, through a long heavy dream of confused time and place, presenting faint glimpses of army surgeons whom he knew, and of faces that had been familiar to his youth – dearest and kindest among them, Mary Marshall's, with a solicitude upon it more like reality than anything he could discern – Lieutenant Richard Doubledick came back to life. To the beautiful life of a calm autumn-evening sunset. To the peaceful life of a fresh quiet room with a large window standing open; a balcony beyond, in which were moving leaves and sweet-smelling flowers; beyond again, the clear sky, with the sun full in his sight, pouring its golden radiance on his bed.

It was so tranquil and so lovely, that he thought he had passed into another world. And he said in a faint voice, 'Taunton, are you near me?'

A face bent over him. Not his; his mother's.

'I came to nurse you. We have nursed you, many weeks. You were moved here, long ago. Do you remember nothing?'

'Nothing.'

The lady kissed his cheek, and held his hand, soothing him.

'Where is the regiment? What has happened? Let me call you mother. What has happened, mother?'

'A great victory, dear. The war is over, and the regiment was the bravest in the field.'

His eyes kindled, his lips trembled, he sobbed, and the tears ran down his face. He was very weak: too weak to move his hand.

'Was it dark just now?' he asked presently.

'No.'

'It was only dark to me? Something passed away, like a black shadow. But, as it went, and the sun – O the blessed sun, how beautiful it is! – touched my face, I thought I saw a light white cloud pass out at the door. Was there nothing that went out?'

She shook her head, and, in a little while, he fell asleep: she still holding his hand, and soothing him.

From that time, he recovered. Slowly, for he had been desperately wounded in the head, and had been shot in the body; but, making some little advance every day. When he had gained sufficient strength to converse as he lay in bed, he soon began to remark that Mrs Taunton always brought him back to his own history. Then, he recalled his preserver's dying words, and thought, 'it comforts her.'

One day, he awoke out of a sleep, refreshed, and asked her to read to him. But, the curtain of the bed, softening the light, which she always drew back when he awoke, that she might see him from her table at the bedside where she sat at work, was held undrawn; and a woman's voice spoke, which was not hers.

'Can you bear to see a stranger?' it said softly. 'Will you like to see a stranger?'

'Stranger!' he repeated. The voice awoke old memories, before the days of Private Richard Doubledick.

'A stranger now, but not a stranger once,' it said in tones that thrilled him. 'Richard, dear Richard, lost through so many years, my name – '

He cried out her name, 'Mary!' and she held him in her arms, and his head lay on her bosom.

'I am not breaking a rash vow, Richard. These are not Mary Marshall's lips that speak. I have another name.'

She was married.

'I have another name, Richard. Did you ever hear it?'

'Never!'

He looked into her face, so pensively beautiful, and wondered at the smile upon it through her tears.

'Think again, Richard. Are you sure you never heard my altered name?'

'Never!'

'Don't move your head to look at me, dear Richard. Let it lie here, while I tell my story. I loved a generous, noble man; loved him with my whole heart; loved him for years and years; loved him faithfully, devotedly; loved him with no hope of return; loved him, knowing nothing of his highest qualities – not even knowing that he was alive. He was a brave soldier. He was honoured and beloved by thousands of thousands, when the mother of his dear friend found me, and showed me that in all his triumphs he had never forgotten me. He was wounded in a great battle. He was brought, dying, here, into Brussels. I came to watch and tend him, as I would have joyfully gone, with such a purpose, to the dreariest ends of the earth. When he knew no one else, he knew me. When he suffered most, he bore his sufferings barely murmuring, content to rest his head where yours rests now. When he lay at the point of death, he married me, that he might call me Wife before he died. And the name, my dear love, that I took on that forgotten night – '

'I know it now!' he sobbed. 'The shadowy remembrance strengthens. It is come back. I thank Heaven that my mind is quite restored! My Mary, kiss me; lull this weary head to rest, or I shall die of gratitude. His parting words are fulfilled. I see Home again!'

Well! They were happy. It was a long recovery, but they were happy through it all. The snow had melted on the ground, and the birds were singing in the leafless thickets of the early spring, when those three were first able to ride out together, and when people flocked about the open carriage to cheer and congratulate Captain Richard Doubledick.

But, even then, it became necessary for the Captain, instead of returning to England, to complete his recovery in the cli-mate of Southern France. They found a spot upon the Rhone, within a ride of the old town of Avignon and within view of its broken bridge, which was all they could desire; they lived there, together, six months; then returned to England. Mrs Taunton growing old after three years – though not so old as that her bright dark eyes were dimmed – and remembering that her strength had been benefited by the change, resolved to go back for a year to those parts. So, she went with a faithful servant, who had often carried her son in his arms; and she was to be rejoined and escorted home, at the year's end, by Captain Richard Doubledick.

She wrote regularly to her children (as she called them now), and they to her. She went to the neighbourhood of Aix; and there, in their own chateau near the farmer's house she rented, she grew into intimacy with a family belonging to that part of France. The intimacy began, in her often meeting among the vineyards a pretty child: a girl with a most compassionate heart, who was never tired of listening to the solitary English lady's stories of her poor son and the cruel wars. The family were as gentle as the child, and at length she came to know them so well, that she accepted their invitation to pass the last month of her residence abroad, under their roof. All this intelligence she wrote home, piecemeal as it came about, from time to time; and, at last, enclosed a polite note from the head of the chateau, soliciting on the occasion of his approaching mission to that neighbourhood, the honour of the company of *cet homme si justement célèbre*,[26] Monsieur le Capitaine Richard Doubledick.

Captain Doubledick; now a hardy handsome man in the full vigour of life, broader across the chest and shoulders than he had ever been before; dispatched a courteous reply, and followed it in person. Travelling through all that extent of country after three years of Peace, he blessed the better days on which the world had fallen. The corn was golden, not drenched in unnatural red; was bound in sheaves for food, not trodden underfoot by men in mortal fight. The smoke rose up from peaceful hearths, not blazing ruins. The carts were laden with the fair fruits of the earth, not with wounds and death. To him who had so often seen the terrible reverse, these things were beautiful indeed, and they brought him in a softened spirit to the old chateau near Aix, upon a deep blue evening.

It was a large chateau of the genuine old ghostly kind, with round towers, and extinguishers and a high leaden roof, and more windows than Aladdin's Palace.[27] The lattice blinds were all thrown open, after the heat of the day, and there were glimpses of rambling walls and corridors within. Then, there were immense outbuildings fallen into partial decay, masses of dark trees, terrace-gardens, balustrades; tanks of water, too weak to play and too dirty to work; statues, weeds, and thickets of iron-railing that seemed to have overgrown themselves like the shrubberies, and to have branched out in all manner of wild shapes. The entrance doors stood open, as doors often do in that country when the heat of the day is past; and the Captain saw no bell or knocker, and walked in.

He walked into a lofty stone hall, refreshingly cool and gloomy after the glare of a Southern day's travel. Extending along the four sides of this hall, was a gallery, leading to suites of rooms; and it was lighted from the top. Still, no bell was to be seen.

'Faith,' said the Captain, halting, ashamed of the clanking of his boots, 'this is a ghostly beginning!'

He started back, and felt his face turn white. In the gallery, looking down at him, stood the French officer: the officer whose picture he had carried in his mind so long and so far. Compared with the original, at last – in every lineament how like it was!

He moved, and disappeared, and Captain Richard Double-dick heard his steps coming quickly down into the hall. He entered through an archway. There was a bright, sudden look upon his face. Much such a look as it had worn in that fatal moment.

Monsieur le Capitaine Richard Doubledick? Enchanted to receive him! A thousand apologies! The servants were all out in the air. There was a little fête among them in the garden. In effect, it was the fête day of my daughter, the little cherished and protected of Madame Taunton.

He was so gracious and so frank, that Monsieur le Capitaine Richard Doubledick could not withhold his hand. 'It is the hand of a brave Englishman,' said the French officer, retaining it while he spoke. 'I could respect a brave Englishman, even as my foe; how much more as my friend! I, also, am a soldier.'

'He has not remembered me, as I have remembered him; he did not take such note of my face, that day, as I took of his,' thought Captain Richard Doubledick. 'How shall I tell him!'

The French officer conducted his guest into a garden, and presented him to his wife: an engaging and beautiful woman, sitting with Mrs Taunton in a whimsical old-fashioned pavilion. His daughter, her fair young face beaming with joy, came running to embrace him; and there was a boy-baby to tumble down among the orange-trees on the broad steps, in making for his father's legs. A multitude of children-visitors were dancing to sprightly music; and all the servants and peasants about the chateau were dancing too. It was a scene of innocent happiness that might have been invented for the climax of the scenes of Peace which had soothed the captain's journey.

He looked on, greatly troubled in his mind, until a re-sounding bell rang, and the French officer begged to show him his rooms. They went upstairs into the gallery from which the officer had looked down; and Monsieur le Capitaine Richard Doubledick was cordially welcomed to a grand outer chamber, and a smaller one within, all clocks, and draperies, and hearths, and brazen dogs, and tiles, and cool devices, and elegance, and vastness.

'You were at Waterloo,' said the French officer.

'I was,' said Captain Richard Doubledick. 'And at Badajos.'

Left alone with the sound of his own stern voice in his ears, he sat down to consider, What shall I do, and how shall I tell him? At that time, unhappily, many deplorable duels had been fought between English and French officers, arising out of the recent war; and these duels, and how to avoid this officer's hospitality, were the uppermost thought in Captain Richard Doubledick's mind.

He was thinking, and letting the time run out in which he should have dressed for dinner, when Mrs Taunton spoke to him outside the door, asking if he could give her the letter he had brought from Mary? 'His mother above all,' the Captain thought. 'How shall I tell *her*?'

'You will form a friendship with your host, I hope,' said Mrs Taunton, whom he hurriedly admitted, 'that will last for life. He is so true-hearted and so generous, Richard, that you can hardly fail to esteem one another. If He had been spared,' she kissed (not without tears) the locket in which she wore his hair, 'he would have appreciated him with his own magnanimity, and would have been truly happy that the evil days were past, which made such a man his enemy.'

She left the room; and the Captain walked, first to one window whence he could see the dancing in the garden, then to another window whence he could see the smiling prospect and the peaceful vineyards.

'Spirit of my departed friend,' said he, 'is it through thee, these better thoughts are rising in my mind! Is it thou who hast shown me, all the way I have been drawn to meet this man, the blessings of the altered time! Is it thou who hast sent thy stricken mother to me, to stay my angry hand! Is it from thee the whisper comes, that this man did his duty as thou didst – and as I did, through thy guidance, which has wholly saved me, here on earth – and that he did no more!'

He sat down, with his head buried in his hands, and, when he rose up, made the second strong resolution of his life: That neither to the French officer, nor to the mother of his departed friend, nor to any soul while either of the two was living, would he breathe what only he knew. And when he touched that French officer's glass with his own, that day at dinner, he secretly forgave him in the name of the Divine Forgiver of injuries.

Here, I ended my story as the first Poor Traveller. But, if I had told it now, I could have added that the time has since come when the son of Major Richard Doubledick and the son of that French officer, friends as their fathers were before them, fought side by side in one cause: with their respective nations, like long-divided brothers whom the better times have brought together, fast united.

THE SECOND POOR TRAVELLER
[by George A. Sala]

I am, by trade (said the man with his arm in a sling), a shipwright. I am recovering from an unlucky chop that one of my mates gave me with an adze.[28] When I am all right again, I shall get taken on in Chatham Yard.[29] I have nothing else in particular to tell of myself, so I'll tell a bit of a story of a seaport town.

Acon-Virlaz the jeweller sat in his shop on the Common Hard of Belleriport smoking his evening pipe. Business was tolerably brisk in Belleriport just then. The great three-decker the Blunderbore (Admiral Pumpkinseed's flag-ship) had just come in from the southern seas with the rest of the squadron, and had been paid off. The big screw line-of-battle ship *Fantail*, Captain Sir Heaver Cole, K.O.B., had got her blue-peter up[30] for Kamschatka, and her crew had been paid advance wages. The Dundrum war steamer was fresh coppering in the graving dock, and her men were enjoying a three weeks' run ashore. The Barracouta, the Calabash, the Skullsmasher, and the Nosering had returned from the African station with lots of prize money from captured slavers.[31] The Jollyport division of Royal Marines – who had plenty of money to spend, and spent it, too, – occupied the Marine barracks. The Ninety-eighth Plungers, together with the depot companies of the Fourteenth Royal Screamers, had marched in to relieve the Seventy-third Wrestlers. There was some thought of embodying, for garrison duty, in Belleriport the Seventh or West Swampshire Drabs regiment of Militia. Belleriport was full of sailors, soldiers, and marines. Seven gold-laced cocked hats could be observed on the doorsteps of the George Hotel at one time. Almost every lady's bonnet in the High Street had a military or naval officer's head looking under it. You could scarcely get into Miss Pyebord the pastrycook's shop for midshipmen. There were so many soldiers in the streets, that you were inclined to take the whole of the population of Belleriport for lobsters, and to imagine that half of them were boiled and the other half waiting to be. The Common Hard was as soft as a feather bed with sailors. Lieutenant Hook at the Rendezvous was busy all day enrolling ABs, ordinaries, and stout lads.[32] The Royal Grubbington victualling yard was turning out thousands of barrels of salt beef and pork and sea biscuits per diem. Huge guns were being hoisted on board ship; seaman-riggers, caulkers, carpenters, and shipwrights, were all some hundreds of degrees busier than bees; and sundry gentlemen in the dockyard, habited in simple suits of drab, marked with the broad arrow – with striped stockings and glazed hats, and after whose personal safety sentinels with fixed bayonets and warders in oilskin coats affectionately looked – were busy too, in their way: dragging about chain-cables, blocks and spars,[33] and loads of timber, steadily but sulkily; and, in their close-shaven, beetle-browed countenances, evincing a silent but profound disgust.

Acon-Virlaz had not done so badly during Belleriport's recent briskness. He was a jeweller; and sold watches, rings, chains, bracelets, snuffboxes, brooches, shirt studs, sleeve-buttons, pencil cases, and true lovers' knots. But, his trade in jewels did not interfere with his also vending hammocks, telescopes, sou'-wester hats, lime juice, maps, charts and logbooks, Guernsey shirts,[34] clasp knives, pea-coats, preserved meats, razors, swinging lamps, sea chests, dancing-pumps, eyeglasses, waterproof overalls, patent blacking, and silk pocket handkerchiefs emblazoned with the flags of all nations. Nor did his dealings in these articles prevent him from driving a very tidy little business in the purchase of gold dust, elephants' teeth, feathers and bandanas, from home-returned sailors; nor (so the censorious said) from deriving some pretty little profits from the cashing of seamen's advance notes, and the discounting of the acceptances of the officers of her majesty's army and navy;[35] nor (so the downright libellous asserted) from doing a little in the wine line, and a little in the picture line, and a good deal, when occasion required it, in the crimp line.[36]

Acon-Virlaz sat in his shop on the Common Hard of Belleriport smoking his evening pipe. It was in the back shop that Acon-Virlaz sat. Above his head, hung the hammocks, the pilot-trowsers[37] narrow at the knees and wide at the ankles, the swinging lamps, and the waterproof overalls. The front shop loomed dimly through a grove of pea-coats, sou'-wester hats, Guernsey shirts, and cans of preserved meat. One little gas jet in the back shop – for the front gas was not yet lighted – flickered on the heterogeneous articles hanging and heaped up together all around. The gas just tipped with light the brass knobs of the drawers which ran round all the four sides of the shop, tier above tier, and held Moses knows how many more treasures of watchmaking, tailoring, and outfitting. The gas just defined by feebly-shining threads, the salient lines and angles of a great iron safe in one corner; and finally the gas just gleamed – twinkled furtively, like a magpie looking into a marrow bone – upon the heap of jewellery collected upon the great slate-covered counter in Acon-Virlaz's back shop.

The counter was covered with slate; for, upon it Acon-Virlaz loved to chalk his calculations. It was ledger, day-book, and journal, all in one. The little curly-headed Jew boy who was clerk, shopman, messenger, and assistant-measurer in the tailoring department of the establishment, would as soon have thought of eating roast sucking-pig beneath Acon-Virlaz's nose,[38] as of wiping, dusting, or, indeed, touching the sacred slate counter without special permission and authority from Acon-Virlaz himself.

By the way, it was not by that name that the jeweller and outfitter was known in Belleriport. He went by a simpler, homelier, shorter appellation: Moses, Levy, Sheeny[39] – what you will; it does not much matter which; for most of the Hebrew nation have an inner name as well as an inner and richer life.

Acon-Virlaz was a little, plump, round, black-eyed, red-lipped, blue-bearded man. Age had begun to discount his head, and had given him sixty per cent of gray hairs. Atop he was bald, and wore a little skullcap. He had large fat hands, all creased and tumbled, as if his skin were too large for him; and, on one forefinger, he wore a great cornelian signet-ring,[40] about which there were all sorts of legends. Miriam, his daughter, said – but what have I to do with Miriam, his daughter? She does not enter into this history at all.

The evening pipe that Acon-Virlaz was smoking was very mild and soothing. The blue haze went curling softly upwards, and seemed to describe pleasant figures of £ s. d. as it ascended. Through the grove, across the front shop, Acon-Virlaz could see little specks of gas from the lamps in the street; could hear Barney, his little clerk and shop boy, softly whistling as he kept watch and ward upon the watches in the front window and the habiliments exposed for sale outside; could hear the sounds of a fiddle from the Admiral Nelson next door, where the men-of-warsmen were dancing; could, by a certain, pleasant, subtle smell from regions yet farther back, divine that Mrs Virlaz (her father was a Bar-Galli, and worth hills of gold) was cooking something nice for supper.

From the pleasures of his pipe Acon-Virlaz turned to the pleasures of his jewellery. It lay there on the slate-covered counter, rich and rare. Big diamonds, rubies, opals, emeralds, sapphires, amethysts, topazes, turquoises, and pearls. By the jewels lay gold. Gold in massy chains, in mourning rings, in massy bracelets, in chased snuffboxes – in gold snuff too – that is in dingy, dull dust from the Guinea coast; in flakes and misshapen lumps from the mine; in toy watches, in brave chronometers, in lockets, vinaigrettes,[41] brooches, and such woman's gear. The voice of the watches was dumb; the little flasks were scentless; but, how much beauty, life, strength, power, lay in these coloured baubles! Acon-Virlaz sighed.

Here, a little clock in the front shop, which nestled ordinarily in the midst of a wilderness of boots, and thought apparently a great deal more of itself than its size warranted, after a prodigious deal of running down, gasping, and clucking, struck nine. Acon-Virlaz laid down his pipe, and turning the gas a little higher, was about calling out to Mrs Virlaz, that daughter of Bar-Galli (she was very stout, and fried fish in sky-blue satin), to know what she had got for supper, when a dark body became mistily apparent in the recesses of the grove of Guernsey shirts and sou'-westers, shutting out the view of the distant specks of gas in the street beyond. At the same time, a voice, that seemed to run upon a tramway, so smooth and sliding was it, said, three or four times over, 'How is tonight with you, Mr Virlaz, – how is it with you this beautiful night? Aha!'

The voice and the body belonged to a gentleman of Mr Virlaz's persuasion, who was stout and large, and very elastic in limb, and very voluble in delivery, in the which there was, I may remark, a tendency to reiteration, and an oily softness (inducing an idea that the tramway I mentioned had been sedulously greased), and a perceptible lisp. Mr Virlaz's friend rubbed his hands (likewise smooth and well-greased) continually. He was somewhat loosely jointed, which caused him to wag his head from side to side as he talked, after the fashion of an image; and his face would have been a great deal handsomer if his complexion had not been quite so white and pasty, and his eyes not quite so pink, and both together not quite so like a suet pudding with two raisins in it.[42] Mr Virlaz's friend's name was Mr Ben-Daoud, and he came from Westhampton, where he discounted bills[43] and sold clocks.

'Take a seat, Ben,' said the jeweller, when he had recognised his friend and shaken hands with him; 'Mrs V. will be down directly. All well at home? Take a pipe?'

'I will just sit down a little minute, and thank you, Mr Virlaz,' Ben-Daoud answered volubly; 'and all are well but little Zeeky, who has thrushes,[44] and has swoollen, the dear child, much since yesterday; but beg Mrs Virlaz not to disturb herself for me, – for I am not long here, and will not take a pipe, having a cold, and being about to go a long journey tomorrow. Aha!'

All this, Mr Ben-Daoud said with the extreme volubility which I have noticed, and in the exact order in which his words are set down, but without any vocal punctuation. There was considerable doubt among the people as to Mr Ben-Daoud's nationality. Some said that he came from Poland; others, that he hailed from Frankfort-on-the-Maine; some inclined to the belief that Amsterdam, in Holland, was his natal place; some, that Gibraltar had given him birth, or the still more distant land of Tangier. At all events, of whatsoever nation he was, or if not of any, he was for all Jewry, and knew the time of the day remarkably well. He had been in the rabbit skin line of business before he took to selling clocks, to which he added, when regiments were in garrison, at Westhampton, the art of discounting.

'Going on a journey, eh, Ben?' asked Acon-Virlaz. 'Business?'

'Oh, business of course, Mr Virlaz,' his friend replied. 'Always business. I have some little moneys to look up, and some little purchases to make, and, indeed, humbly wish to turn a little penny; for, I have very many heavy calls to meet next month, – a little bill or two of mine you hold, by the way, among the rest, Mr Virlaz.'

'True,' the jeweller said, rather nervously, and putting his hand on a great leathern portfolio in his breast pocket, in which he kept his acceptances; 'and shall you be long gone, Mr Daoud?'

This 'Mr Daoud,' following upon the former familiar 'Ben,' was said without sternness, but spoke the creditor awakened to his rights. It seemed to say, 'Smoke, drink, and be merry till your "accepted payable at such a date" comes due; but pay then, or I'll sell you up like death.'

Mr Ben-Daoud seemed to have an inkling of this; for, he wagged his head, rubbed his hands, and answered, more volubly than ever, 'Oh, as to that, Mr Virlaz, dear sir, my journey is but of two days lasting. I shall be back the day after tomorrow, and with something noticeable in the way of diamonds. Aha!'

'Diamonds!' exclaimed Acon-Virlaz, glancing towards the drawer where his jewels were; for you may be sure he had swept them all away into safety before his friend had completed his entrance. 'Diamonds! Where are you going for diamonds, Ben?'

'Why, to the great fair that is held tomorrow, Mr Virlaz, as well you know.'

'Fair, Ben? Is there any fair tomorrow near Belleriport?'

'Why, bless my heart, Mr Virlaz,' Ben-Daoud responded, holding up his fat hands; 'can it be that you, so respectable and noticeable a man among our people, don't know that tomorrow is the great jewel fair that is held once in every hundred years, at which diamonds, rubies, and all other pretty stones are sold cheap – cheap as dirt, my dear – a hundred thousand guineas-worth for sixpence, one may say. Your grandfather must have been there, and well he made his market, you may be sure. Aha! Good man!'

'I never heard of such a thing,' gasped Acon-Virlaz, perfectly amazed and bewildered. 'And what do you call this fair?'

'Why, Sky Fair! As well you should know, dear sir.'

'Sky Fair?' repeated the jeweller.

'Sky Fair,' answered Ben-Daoud.

'But whereabouts is it?'

'Come here,' the voluble man said. He took hold of Acon-Virlaz by the wrist, and led him through the grove of pea-coats into the front shop; through the front shop into the open street; and then pointing upwards, he directed the gaze of the Jew to where, in the otherwise unillumined sky, there was shining one solitary star.

'Don't it look pretty?' he asked, sinking his voice into a confidential whisper. 'Don't it look like a diamond, and glitter and twinkle as if some of our people the lapidaries[45] in Amsterdam had cut it into faces. That's where Sky Fair is, Mr Virlaz. Aha!'

'And you are going there tomorrow?' Acon-Virlaz asked, glancing uneasily at his companion.

'Of course I am,' Ben-Daoud replied, 'with my little bag of money to make my little purchases. And saving your presence, dear sir, I think you will be a great fool if you don't come with me, and make some little purchases too. For, diamonds, Mr

Virlaz, are not so easily come by every day, as in Sky Fair; and a hundred years is a long time to wait before one can make another such bargain.'

'I'll come, Ben,' the jeweller cried, enthusiastically. 'I'll come; and if ever I can do you any little obligation in the way of moneys, I will.' And he grasped the hand of Ben-Daoud, who sold clocks and discounted.

'Why, that's right,' the other returned. 'And I'll come for you at eight o'clock tomorrow, punctually; so get your little bag of money and your nightcap and a comb ready.'

'But,' the jeweller asked, with one returning tinge of suspicion, 'how are we to get there, Ben?'

'Oh,' replied Mr Ben-Daoud, cooly, 'we'll have a shay.'[46]

Sky Fair! – diamonds! – cheap bargains! Acon-Virlaz could think of nothing else all the time of supper; which was something very nice indeed in the fish way, and into the cooking of which oil entered largely. He was so preoccupied, that Mrs Virlaz, and Miriam his daughter, who had large eyes and a coral necklace (for weekdays), were fain to ask him the cause thereof; and he, like a good and tender husband and father as he was (and as most Hebrews, to their credit, are), told them of Ben-Daoud's marvellous story, and of his intended journey.

The next morning, as the clock struck eight, the sound of wheels was heard before Acon-Virlaz's door in the Common Hard of Belleriport, and a handful of gravel was playfully thrown against the first-floor window by the hands of Ben-Daoud of Westhampton.

But it needed no gravel, no noise of wheels, no striking of clocks, to awaken Acon-Virlaz. He had been up and dressed since six o'clock; and, leaving Mrs Virlaz peacefully and soundly sleeping; and hastily swallowing some hot coffee prepared by Barney the lad (to whom he issued strict injunctions concerning the conduct of the warehouse during the day); he descended into the street, and was affectionately hailed by his fellow voyager to Sky Fair.

The seller of clocks sat in the 'shay' of which he had spoken to Acon-Virlaz. It was a dusky little concern, very loose on its springs, and worn and rusty in its gear. As to the animal that drew it, Mr Ben-Daoud mentioned by the way that it was a discount pony; having been taken as an equivalent for cash in numberless bills negotiated in the Westhampton garrison, and had probably been worth, in his time, considerably more than his weight in gold.

Said pony, if he was a rum 'un to look at – which, indeed, he was, being hairy where he should have been smooth, and having occasional bald places as though he were in the habit of scratching himself with his hoofs – which hoofs, coupled with his whity-brown ankles, gave him the appearance of having indifferent bluchers and dirty white socks on – was a good 'un to go. So remarkably good was he in going, that he soon left behind, the high street of Belleriport, where the shop boys were sleepily taking down the shutters; where housemaids were painfully elaborating the doorsteps with hearthstones, to be soiled by the first visitor's dirty boots (such is the way of the world); where the milkman was making his early morning calls, and the night policemen were going home from duty; and the third lieutenant of the Blunderbore – who had been ashore on leave, and was a little shaken about the eyes still – was hastening to catch the 'beef-boat'[47] to convey him to his ship. Next, the town itself did the pony leave behind: the outskirts, the outlying villages, the ruined stocks and deserted pound, the Port-Admiral's villa: all these he passed, running as fast as a constable, or a bill,[48] until he got at last into a broad white road, which Acon-Virlaz never remembered to have seen before; a road with a high hedge on either side, and to which there seemed to be no end.

Mr Ben-Daoud drove the pony in first-rate style. His head and the animal's wagged in concert; and the more he flourished his whip, the more the pony went; and both seemed to like it. The great white road sent up no dust. Its stones, if stones it had, never grated nor gave out a sound beneath the wheels of the 'shay.' It was only very white and broad, and seemed to have no end.

Not always white, however; for, as they progressed, it turned in colour first milky-grey, then what schoolboys call, in connection with the fluid served out to them at breakfast time, sky-blue; then a deep, vivid, celestial blue. And the high hedge on either side melted by degrees into the same hue; and Acon-Virlaz began to feel curiously feathery about the body, and breezy about the lungs. He caught hold of the edge of the 'shay,' as though he were afraid of falling over. He shut his eyes from time to time, as though he were dizzy. He began to fancy that he was in the sky.

'There is Sky Fair, Mr Virlaz!' Ben-Daoud suddenly said, pointing ahead with his whip.

At that moment, doubtless through the superior attractions of Sky Fair, the dusky 'shay' became of so little account to Acon-Virlaz as to disappear entirely from his sight and mind, though he had left his nightcap and comb (his little bag of money was safe in his side-pocket, trust him), on the cushion. At the same moment it must have occurred to the discount pony to put himself out at living in some very remote corner of creation, for, he vanished altogether too; and Acon-Virlaz almost fancied that he saw the beast's collar fall fifty thousand fathoms five, true as a plumb-line,[49] into space; and the reins, which but a moment before Ben-Daoud had held, flutter loosely away, like feathers.

He found himself treading upon a hard, loose, gritty surface, which, on looking down, appeared like diamond-dust.

'Which it is,' Mr Ben-Daoud explained, when Acon-Virlaz timidly asked him. 'Cheap as dirt here! Capital place to bring your cast-iron razors to be sharpened, Mr Virlaz.'

The jeweller felt inclined for the moment, to resent this pleasantry as somewhat personal; for, to say truth, the razors in which he dealt were not of the primest steel.

There was a great light. The brightest sunlight that Acon-Virlaz had ever seen was but a poor farthing candle compared to this resplendency. There was a great gate through which they had to pass to the fair. The gate seemed to Acon-Virlaz as if all the jewellery and wrought gold in the world had been half-fused, half-welded together, into one monstrous arabesque or trelliswork. There was a little porter's lodge by the gate, and a cunning-looking little man by it, with a large bunch of keys at his girdle. The thing seemed impossible and ridiculous, yet Acon-Virlaz could not help fancying that he had seen the cunning little porter before, and, of all places in the world, in London, at the lock-up house in Cursitor Street, Chancery Lane, kept by Mr Mephibosheth, to whose red-headed little turnkey, Benjy, he bore an extraordinary resemblance.

Who is to tell of the glories of Sky Fair? Who, indeed, unless he had a harp of gold strung with diamonds? Who is to tell of the long lines of dazzlingly white booths, hundreds, if not thousands, if not millions, of miles in extent, where jewels of surpassing size and purest water were sold by the peck, like peas; by the pound, like spice nuts; by the gallon, like table beer? Who is to tell of the swings, the roundabouts, the throwing of sticks, each stick surmounted by a diamond as big as an ostrich egg; the live armadillos with their jewelled scales; the scratchers, corruscating like meteors; the gingerbread kings and queens; the whole fun of the fair, one dazzling, blinding, radiating mass of gold and gems!

It was not Acon-Virlaz who could tell much about these wondrous things in after days, for he was too occupied with his little bag of money, and his little fairings. Ben-Daoud had spoken the truth: diamonds were as cheap as dirt in Sky Fair. In an inconceivably short space of time, and by the expenditure of a few halfpence, the jeweller had laid in a stock of precious stones. But, he was not satisfied with pockets-full, bags-full, hat-full, of unset, uncut gems. There were heaps of jewelled trinkets, chains, bracelets, rings, piled up for sale. He hankered after these. He bought heaps of golden rings. He decorated his wrists and ankles with bracelets and bangles enough for a Bayadere.[50] He might have been a dog, for the collars round his neck. He might have been an Ambrose Gwynnett[51] hung in chains, for the profusion of those ornaments in gold, with which he loaded himself. And then he went in for solid services of plate, and might have been a butler or a philanthropist, for the piles of ewers, salvers, candelabra, and goblets which he accumulated in his hands, under his arms, on his head. More gold! more jewels! More – more –

Till a bell began to ring, – a loud, clanging, voiceful golden bell, carried by a shining bellman, and the clapper of which was one huge diamond. The thousands of people who, a moment before, had been purchasing jewels and gold, no sooner heard the bell than they began to scamper like mad towards the gate; and, at the same time, Acon-Virlaz heard the bellman making proclamation that Sky Fair would close in ten minutes time, and that every man, woman, or child found within the precincts of the fair, were it only for the thousandth part of the tithe of a moment after the clock had struck Twelve, would be turned into stone for a hundred years.

Till the men, women, and children from every nation under the sun (he had not observed them until now, so intent had he been on his purchases), came tearing past him; treading on his toes, bruising his ribs, jostling him, pushing him from side to side, screaming to him with curses to move on quicker, or to get out of the way. But, he could not move on quicker. His gold stuck to him. His jewels weighed him down. Invisible clogs seemed to attach themselves to his feet. He kept dropping his precious wares, and, for the life of him, could not refrain from stopping to pick them up; in doing which he dropped more.

Till Mr Ben-Daoud passed him with a girdle of big diamonds, tied round his waist in a blue bird's-eye handkerchief, like a professional pedestrian.

Till the great bell from ringing intermittent peals kept up one continuous clang. Till a clock above, like a catherine wheel,[52] which Acon-Virlaz had not before noticed, began to let off rockets of minutes, Roman candles of seconds. Till the bellman's proclamation merged into one sustained roar of Oh yes! Oh yes! Till the red-headed gatekeeper, who was like Mr Mephibosheth's turnkey, gave himself up to an unceasing scream of 'All out! All out!' whirling his keys above his head, so that they scattered sparks and flakes of fire all around.

Till fifty thousand other bells began to clang, and fifty million other voices to scream. Till all at once there was silence, and the clock began to strike slowly, sadly, One, two, three, four – to Twelve.

Acon-Virlaz was within a few feet of the gate when the fatal clock began to strike. By a desperate effort he cast aside the load of plate which impeded his movements. He tore off his diamond-laden coat; he cast his waistcoat to the winds, and plunged madly into the throng that blocked up the entrance.

To find himself too late. The great gates closed with a heavy shock, and Acon-Virlaz reeled away from them in the rebound, bruised, bleeding, and despairing. He was too late. Sky Fair was closed, and he was to be turned into stone for a hundred years.

The red-headed doorkeeper (who by the way squinted abominably) was leaning with his back to the gate, drumming with his keys on the bars.

'It's a beautiful day to be indoors,' he said, consolingly. 'It's bitter cold outside.'

Acon-Virlaz shuddered. He felt his heart turning into stone within him. He fell on his knees before the red-headed door-keeper; and with tears, sobs, groans, entreated him to open the gate. He offered him riches, he offered him the hand of Miriam his large-eyed daughter: all for one turn of the key in the lock of the gate of Sky Fair.

'Can't be done,' the doorkeeper remarked, shaking his head. 'Till Sky Fair opens again, you can't be let out.'

Again and again did the jeweller entreat, until he at last appeared to make an impression on the red-headed janitor.

'Well, I'll tell you what I can do for you, old gentleman,' he said: 'I daren't open the gate for my life; but there's a window in my lodge; and if you choose to take your chance of jumping out of it (it isn't far to fall) you can.'

Acon-Virlaz, uttering a confused medley of thanks, was about to rush into the lodge, when the gatekeeper laid his hand upon his arm.

'By the way, mister,' he said, 'you may as well give me that big signet ring on your finger, as a token to remind you of all the fine things you promised me when I come your way.'

The jeweller hastily plucked off the desired trinket, and gave it to his red-headed deliverer. Then, he darted into the narrow, dark porter's lodge, overturned a round table, on which was the doorkeeper's dinner (it smelt very much like liver and bacon), and clambered up to a very tall, narrow window.

He leaned his hands on the sill, and thrusting his head out to see how far he had to jump, descried, immediately, beneath him the dusty shay, the discount pony, and Mr Ben-Daoud with a lighted cigar in his mouth and the reins in his hand, just ready to start.

'Hold hard!' screamed Acon-Virlaz. 'Hold hard! Ben, my dear friend, my old friend: hold hard, and take me in!'

Mr Ben-Daoud's reply was concise but conclusive:

'Go to Bermondsey,'[53] he said, and whipped his pony.

The miserable man groaned aloud in despair; for the voice of the doorkeeper urged him to be quick about it, if he was going to jump; and he felt, not only his heart, but his limbs, becoming cold and stony.

Shutting his eyes and clenching his teeth, he jumped and fell, down, down into space. According to his own calculations, he must have fallen at least sixty thousand miles and for six months in succession; but, according to Mrs Acon-Virlaz and Miriam his large-eyed daughter, he only fell from his armchair into the fireplace, striking his head against the tongs as he fell; having come home a little while before, with no such thing about him as his beautiful seal-ring; and being slightly the worse for liquor, not to say drunk.

THE THIRD POOR TRAVELLER
[by Adelaide Anne Procter]

You wait my story, next? Ah, well!
Such marvels as you two have told
You must not think that I can tell;
For I am only twelve years old.
Ere long I hope I shall have been
On my first voyage, and wonders seen.
Some princess I may help to free
From pirates on a far-off sea;
Or, on some desert isle be left,
Of friends and shipmates all bereft.

    For the first time I venture forth,
From our blue mountains of the north.
My kinsman kept the lodge that stood
Guarding the entrance near the wood,
By the stone gateway gray and old,
With quaint devices carved about,
And broken shields; while dragons bold
Glared on the common world without;
And the long trembling ivy spray
Half hid the centuries' decay.
In solitude and silence grand
The castle towered above the land:
The castle of the Earl, whose name
(Wrapped in old bloody legends) came
Down through the times when Truth and Right
Bent down to armèd Pride and Might.
He owned the country far and near;
And, for some weeks in every year,

(When the brown leaves were falling fast
And the long, lingering autumn passed),
He would come down to hunt the deer,
With hound and horse in splendid pride.
The story lasts the live-long year,
The peasant's winter evening fills,
When he is gone and they abide
In the lone quiet of their hills.

    I longed, too, for the happy night,
When all with torches flaring bright
The crowding villagers would stand,
A patient, eager, waiting band,
Until the signal ran like flame
'They come!' and, slackening speed, they came.
Outriders first, in pomp and state,
Pranced on their horses thro' the gate;
Then the four steeds as black as night,
All decked with trappings blue and white,
Drew thro' the crowd that opened wide,
The Earl and Countess side by side.
The stern grave Earl, with formal smile
And glistening eyes and stately pride,
Could ne'er my childish gaze beguile
From the fair presence by his side.
The lady's soft sad glance, her eyes
(Like stars that shone in summer skies),
Her pure white face so calmly bent,
With gentle greetings round her sent;
Her look, that always seemed to gaze
Where the blue past had closed again
Over some happy shipwrecked days,

With all their freight of love and pain.
She did not even seem to see
The little lord upon her knee.
And yet he was like angel fair,
With rosy cheeks and golden hair,
That fell on shoulders white as snow.
But the blue eyes that shone below
His clustering rings of auburn curls,
Were not his mother's, but the Earl's.

I feared the Earl, so cold and grim,
I never dared be seen by him.
When thro' our gate he used to ride,
My kinsman Walter bade me hide;
He said he was so stern.
So, when the hunt came past our way,
I always hasten'd to obey,
Until I heard the bugles play
The notes of their return.
But she – my very heart-strings stir
Whene'er I speak or think of her –
The whole wide world could never see
A noble lady such as she,
So full of angel charity.

Strange things of her our neighbours told
In the long winter evenings cold,
Around the fire. They would draw near
And speak half-whispering, as in fear:
As if they thought the Earl could hear
Their treason 'gainst his name.
They thought the story that his pride

Had stooped to wed a low-born bride,
A stain upon his fame.
Some said 'twas false; there could not be
Such blot on his nobility:
But others vowed that they had heard
The actual story word for word,
From one who well my lady knew,
And had declared the story true.

In a far village, little known,
She dwelt – so ran the tale – alone.
A widowed bride, yet, oh! so bright,
Shone through the mist of grief, her charms;
They said it was the loveliest sight, –
She with her baby in her arms.
The Earl, one summer morning, rode
By the sea-shore where she abode;
Again he came, – that vision sweet
Drew him reluctant to her feet.
Fierce must the struggle in his heart
Have been, between his love and pride,
Until he chose that wondrous part,
To ask her to become his bride.
Yet, ere his noble name she bore,
He made her vow that nevermore
She would behold her child again,
But hide his name and hers from men.
The trembling promise duly spoken,
All links of the low past were broken,
And she arose to take her stand
Amid the nobles of the land.

Then all would wonder, – could it be
That one so lowly born as she,
Raised to such height of bliss, should seem
Still living in some weary dream?
'Tis true she bore with calmest grace
The honours of her lofty place,
Yet never smiled, in peace or joy,
Not even to greet her princely boy.
She heard, with face of white despair,
The cannon thunder through the air,
That she had given the Earl an heir.
Nay, even more (they whispered low,
As if they scarce durst fancy so),
That, through her lofty wedded life,
No word, no tone betrayed the wife.
Her look seemed ever in the past;
Never to him it grew more sweet;
The self-same weary glance she cast
Upon the grey-hound at her feet,
As upon him, who bade her claim
The crowning honour of his name.

This gossip, if old Walter heard,
He checked it with a scornful word:
I never durst such tales repeat;
He was too serious and discreet
To speak of what his lord might do.
Besides, he loved my lady too:
And many a time, I recollect,
They were together in the wood;
He, with an air of grave respect,
And earnest look, uncovered stood.

And though their speech I never heard,
(Save now and then a louder word,)
I saw he spake as none but one
She loved and trusted, durst have done;
For oft I watched them in the shade
That the close forest branches made,
Till slanting golden sunbeams came
And smote the fir-trees into flame,
A radiant glory round her lit,
Then down her white robe seemed to flit,
Gilding the brown leaves on the ground,
And all the feathery ferns around.
While by some gloomy pine she leant
And he in earnest talk would stand,
I saw the tear-drops, as she bent,
Fall on the flowers in her hand.
Strange as it seemed and seems to be,
That one so sad, so cold as she,
Could love a little child like me;
Yet so it was. I never heard
Such tender words as she would say,
Or murmurs, sweeter than a word,
Would breathe upon me as I lay.
While I, in smiling joy, would rest,
For hours, my head upon her breast.
Our neighbours said that none could see
In me the common childish charms,
(So grave and still I used to be,)
And yet she held me in her arms,
In a fond clasp, so close, so tight, –
I often dream of it at night.

She bade me tell her all – no other,
My childish thoughts e're cared to know;
For I – I never knew my mother;
I was an orphan long ago.
And I could all my fancies pour,
That gentle loving face before.
She liked to hear me tell her all;
How that day I had climbed the tree,
To make the largest fir-cones fall;
And how one day I hoped to be
A sailor on the deep blue sea –
She loved to hear it all!

Then wondrous things she used to tell,
Of the strange dreams that she had known.
I used to love to hear them well;
If only for her sweet low tone,
Sometimes so sad, although I knew
That such things never could be true.
One day she told me such a tale
It made me grow all cold and pale,
The fearful thing she told!
Of a poor woman mad and wild
Who coined the life-blood of her child,
Who, tempted by a fiend, had sold
The heart out of her breast for gold.
But, when she saw me frightened seem,
She smiled, and said it was a dream.
How kind, how fair she was; how good
I cannot tell you. If I could
You, too, would love her. The mere thought
Of her great love for me has brought

Tears in my eyes: though far away,
It seems as it were yesterday.
And just as when I look on high
Through the blue silence of the sky,
Fresh stars shine out, and more and more,
Where I could see so few before.
So, the more steadily I gaze
Upon those far-off misty days,
Fresh words, fresh tones, fresh memories start
Before my eyes and in my heart.
I can remember how one day
(Talking in silly childish way)
I said how happy I should be
If I were like her son – as fair,
With just such bright blue eyes as he,
And such long locks of golden hair.
A dark smile on her pale face broke,
And in strange solemn words she spoke:
    'My own, my darling one – no, no!
I love you, far, far better so.
I would not change the look you bear,
Or one wave of your dark brown hair.
The mere glance of your sunny eyes,
Deep in my deepest soul I prize
Above that baby fair!
Not one of all the Earl's proud line
In beauty ever matched with thine.
And, 'tis by thy dark locks thou art
Bound even faster round my heart,
And made more wholly mine!'
And then she paused, and weeping said,
'You are like one who now is dead –

Who sleeps in a far distant grave.
O may God grant that you may be
As noble and as good as he,
As gentle and as brave!'
Then in my childish way I cried,
'The one you tell me of who died,
Was he as noble as the Earl?'
I see her red lips scornful curl,
I feel her hold my hand again
So tightly, that I shrank in pain –
I seem to hear her say,
'He whom I tell you of, who died,
He was so noble and so gay,
So generous and so brave,
That the proud Earl by his dear side
Would look a craven slave.'
She paused; then, with a quivering sigh,
She laid her hand upon my brow:
'Live like him, darling, and so die.
Remember that he tells you now,
True peace, real honour, and content,
In cheerful pious toil abide;
For gold and splendour are but sent
To curse our vanity and pride.'

One day some childish fever pain
Burnt in my veins and fired my brain.
Moaning, I turned from side to side;
And, sobbing in my bed, I cried,
Till night in calm and darkness crept
Around me, and at last I slept.
When suddenly I woke to see

The Lady bending over me.
The drops of cold November rain
Were falling from her long, damp hair;
Her anxious eyes were dim with pain;
Yet she looked wondrous fair.
Arrayed for some great feast she came,
With stones that shone and burnt like flame.
Wound round her neck, like some bright snake,
And set like stars within her hair,
They sparkled so, they seemed to make
A glory everywhere.
I felt her tears upon my face,
Her kisses on my eyes;
And a strange thought I could not trace
I felt within my heart arise;
And, half in feverish pain, I said:
'O if my mother were not dead!'
And Walter bade me sleep; but she
Said, 'Is it not the same to thee
That *I* watch by thy bed?'
I answered her, 'I love you, too;
But it can never be the same:
She was no Countess like to you,
Nor wore such sparkling stones of flame.'
O the wild look of fear and dread!
The cry she gave of bitter woe!
I often wonder what I said
To make her moan and shudder so.

Through the long night she tended me
With such sweet care and charity.
But I should weary you to tell

All that I know and love so well:
Yet one night more stands out alone
With a sad sweetness all its own.

The wind blew loud that dreary night.
Its wailing voice I well remember;
The stars shone out so large and bright
Upon the frosty fir-boughs white:
That dreary night of cold December.
I saw old Walter silent stand,
Watching the soft last flakes of snow
With looks I could not understand
Of strange perplexity and woe.
At last he turned and took my hand,
And said the Countess just had sent
To bid us come; for she would fain
See me once more, before she went
Away, – never to come again.
We came in silence thro' the wood
(Our footfall was the only sound),
To where the great white castle stood,
With darkness shadowing it around.
Breathless, we trod with cautious care
Up the great echoing marble stair;
Trembling, by Walter's hand I held,
Scared by the splendours I beheld:
Now thinking, Should the Earl appear!
Now looking up with giddy fear
To the dim vaulted roof, that spread
Its gloomy arches overhead.
Long corridors we softly past,
(My heart was beating loud and fast)

And reached the Lady's room at last.
A strange faint odour seemed to weigh
Upon the dim and darkened air.
One shaded lamp, with softened ray,
Scarce showed the gloomy splendour there.
The dull red brands were burning low:
And yet a fitful gleam of light,
Would now and then with sudden glow,
Start forth, then sink again in night.
I gazed around, yet half in fear,
Till Walter told me to draw near.
And in the strange and flickering light,
Towards the Lady's bed I crept.
All folded round with snowy white,
She lay (one would have said she slept).
So still the look of that white face,
It seemed as it were carved in stone.
I paused before I dared to place
Within her cold white hand my own.
But, with a smile of sweet surprise,
She turned to me her dreamy eyes;
And slowly, as if life were pain,
She drew me in her arms to lie:
She strove to speak, and strove in vain;
Each breath was like a long-drawn sigh,
The throbs that seemed to shake her breast,
The trembling clasp, so loose, and weak,
At last grew calmer, and at rest;
And then she strove once more to speak:
'My God, I thank thee, that my pain
Of day by day and year by year,
Has not been suffered all in vain,

And I may die while he is near.
I will not fear but that Thy grace
Has swept away my sin and woe,
And sent this little angel face,
In my last hour to tell me so.'
(And here her voice grew faint and low)
'My child where'er thy life may go,
To know that thou art brave and true,
Will pierce the highest heavens through,
And even there my soul shall be
More joyful for this thought of thee.'
She folded her white hands, and stayed,
All cold and silently she lay:
I knelt beside the bed, and prayed
The prayer she used to make me say.
I said it many times, and then
She did not move, but seemed to be
In a deep sleep, nor stirred again.
No sound stirred in the silent room,
Or broke the dim and solemn gloom,
Save when the brands that burnt so low
With noisy fitful gleam of light,
Would spread around a sudden glow,
Then sink in silence and in night.
How long I stood I do not know:
At last poor Walter came, and said
(So sadly) that we now must go,
And whispered, she we loved was dead.
He bade me kiss her face once more,
Then led me sobbing to the door.
I scarcely knew what dying meant,
Yet a strange grief, before unknown,

Weighed on my spirit as we went
And left her lying all alone.

We went to the far North once more,
To seek the well-remembered home,
Where my poor kinsman dwelt before,
Whence now he was too old to roam;
And there six happy years we past,
Happy and peaceful till the last;
When poor old Walter died, and he
Blessed me and said I now might be
A sailor on the deep blue sea.
And so I go; and yet in spite
Of all the joys I long to know;
Though I look onward with delight,
With something of regret I go,
And young or old, on land or sea,
One guiding memory I shall take
Of what She prayed that I might be,
And what I will be for her sake!

THE FOURTH POOR TRAVELLER
[by Wilkie Collins]

Now, first of all, I should like to know what you mean by a story? You mean what other people do? And pray what is that? You know, but you can't exactly tell. I thought so! In the course of a pretty long legal experience, I have never yet met with a party out of my late profession, who was capable of giving a correct definition of anything.

To judge by your looks, I suspect you are amused at my talking of any such thing ever having belonged to me as a profession. Ha! ha! Here I am, with my toes out of my boots, without a shirt to my back or a rap[54] in my pocket, except the fourpence I get out of this charity (against the present administration of which I protest – but that's not the point), and yet not two years ago I was an attorney in large practice in a bursting big country town. I had a house in the High Street. Such a giant of a house that you had to get up six steps to knock at the front door. I had a footman to drive tramps like me off all or any one of my six hearth-stoned steps, if they dared sit down on all or any one of my six hearth-stoned steps; – a footman who would give me into custody now if I tried to shake hands with him in the streets. I decline to answer your questions if you ask me any. How I got into trouble, and dropped down to where I am now, is my secret.

Now, I absolutely decline to tell you a story. But, though I won't tell a story, I am ready to make a statement. A statement is a matter of fact; therefore the exact opposite of a story, which is a matter of fiction. What I am now going to tell you really happened to me.

I served my time – never mind in whose office; and I started in business for myself, in one of our English country

63

towns – I decline stating which. I hadn't a quarter of the capital I ought to have had to begin with; and my friends in the neighbourhood were poor and useless enough, with one exception. That exception was Mr Frank Gatliffe, son of Mr Gatliffe, member for the county, the richest man and the proudest for many a mile round about our parts. – Stop a bit! you man in the corner there; you needn't perk up and look knowing. You won't trace any particulars by the name of Gatliffe. I'm not bound to commit myself or anybody else by mentioning names. I have given you the first that came into my head.

Well! Mr Frank was a staunch friend of mine, and ready to recommend me whenever he got the chance. I had given him a little timely help – for a consideration, of course – in borrowing money at a fair rate of interest: in fact, I had saved him from the Jews. The money was borrowed while Mr Frank was at college. He came back from college, and stopped at home a little while: and then there got spread about all our neighbourhood, a report that he had fallen in love, as the saying is, with his young sister's governess, and that his mind was made up to marry her. – What! you're at it again, my man in the corner! You want to know her name, don't you? What do you think of Smith?

Speaking as a lawyer, I consider Report, in a general way, to be a fool and a liar. But in this case report turned out to be something very different. Mr Frank told me he was really in love, and said upon his honour (an absurd expression which young chaps of his age are always using) he was determined to marry Smith the governess – the sweet darling girl, as *he* called her; but I'm not sentimental, and *I* call her Smith the governess (with an eye, of course, to refreshing the memory of my friend in the corner). Mr Frank's father, being as proud as

Lucifer, said 'No' as to marrying the governess, when Mr Frank wanted him to say 'Yes.' He was a man of business, was old Gatliffe, and he took the proper business course. He sent the governess away with a first-rate character and a spanking present; and then he looked about him to get something for Mr Frank to do. While he was looking about, Mr Frank bolted to London after the governess, who had nobody alive belonging to her to go to but an aunt – her father's sister. The aunt refuses to let Mr Frank in without the squire's permission. Mr Frank writes to his father, and says he will marry the girl as soon as he is of age, or shoot himself. Up to town comes the squire, and his wife, and his daughter; and a lot of sentimentality, not in the slightest degree material to the present statement, takes place among them; and the upshot of it is that old Gatliffe is forced into withdrawing the word No, and substituting the word Yes.

I don't believe he would ever have done it, though, but for one lucky peculiarity in the case. The governess's father was a man of good family – pretty nigh as good as Gatliffe's own. He had been in the army; had sold out; set up as a wine merchant – failed – died: ditto his wife, as to the dying part of it. No relation, in fact, left for the squire to make inquiries about but the father's sister; who had behaved, as old Gatliffe said, like a thoroughbred gentlewoman in shutting the door against Mr Frank in the first instance. So, to cut the matter short, things were at last made up pleasant enough. The time was fixed for the wedding, and an announcement about it – Marriage in High Life and all that – put into the county paper. There was a regular biography, besides, of the governess's father, so as to stop people from talking; a great flourish about his pedigree, and a long account of his services in the army; but not a word, mind ye, of his having turned wine merchant afterwards. Oh, no – not a word about that! I knew it, though, for Mr Frank told me. He hadn't a bit of pride about him. He introduced me to his future wife one day when I met them out walking, and asked me if I did not think he was a lucky fellow. I don't mind admitting that I did, and that I told him so. Ah! but she was one of my sort, was that governess. Stood, to the best of my recollection, five foot four. Good lissome[55] figure, that looked as if it had never been boxed up in a pair of stays. Eyes that made me feel as if I was under a pretty stiff cross-examination the moment she looked at me. Fine red, fresh, kiss-and-come-again sort of lips. Cheeks and complexion – No, my man in the corner, you wouldn't identify her by her cheeks and complexion, if I drew you a picture of them this very moment. She has had a family of children since the time I'm talking of; and her cheeks are a trifle fatter and her complexion is a shade or two redder now, than when I first met her out walking with Mr Frank.

The marriage was to take place on a Wednesday. I decline mentioning the year or the month. I had started as an attorney on my own account – say six weeks, more or less, and was sitting alone in my office on the Monday morning before the wedding day, trying to see my way clear before me and not succeeding particularly well, when Mr Frank suddenly bursts in, as white as any ghost that ever was painted, and says he's got the most dreadful case for me to advise on, and not an hour to lose in acting on my advice.

'Is this in the way of business, Mr Frank?' says I, stopping him just as he was beginning to get sentimental. 'Yes or no, Mr Frank?' rapping my new office paper-knife on the table to pull him up short all the sooner.

'My dear fellow' – he was always familiar with me – 'it's in the way of business, certainly; but friendship – '

I was obliged to pull him up short again and regularly examine him as if he had been in the witness-box, or he would have kept me talking to no purpose half the day.

'Now, Mr Frank,' said I, 'I can't have any sentimentality mixed up with business matters. You please to stop talking, and let me ask questions. Answer in the fewest words you can use. Nod when nodding will do instead of words.'

I fixed him with my eye for about three seconds, as he sat groaning and wriggling in his chair. When I'd done fixing him, I gave another rap with my paper-knife on to the table to startle him up a bit. Then I went on.

'From what you have been stating up to the present time,' says I, 'I gather that you are in a scrape which is likely to interfere seriously with your marriage on Wednesday?' (He nodded, and I cut in again before he could say a word). 'The scrape affects the young lady you are about to marry, and goes back to the period of a certain transaction in which her late father was engaged some years ago?' (He nods, and I cut in once more.) 'There is a party who turned up after seeing the announcement of your marriage in the paper, who is cognisant of what he oughtn't to know, and who is prepared to use his knowledge of the same, to the prejudice of the young lady and of your marriage, unless he receives a sum of money to quiet him? Very well. Now, first of all, Mr Frank, state what you have been told by the young lady herself about the transaction of her late father. How did you first come to have any knowledge of it?'

'She was talking to me about her father one day, so tenderly and prettily, that she quite excited my interest about him,' begins Mr Frank; 'and I asked her, among other things, what had occasioned his death. She said she believed it was distress of mind in the first instance; and added that this distress was

67

connected with a shocking secret, which she and her mother had kept from everybody, but which she could not keep from me, because she was determined to begin her married life by having no secrets from her husband.' Here Mr Frank began to get sentimental again; and I pulled him up short once more with the paper-knife.

'She told me,' Mr Frank went on, 'that the great mistake of her father's life was his selling out of the army and taking to the wine trade. He had no talent for business; things went wrong with him from the first. His clerk, it was strongly suspected, cheated him – '

'Stop a bit,' says I, 'What was that suspected clerk's name?'

'Davager,' says he.

'Davager,' says I, making a note of it. 'Go on, Mr Frank.'

'His affairs got more and more entangled,' says Mr Frank; 'he was pressed for money in all directions; bankruptcy, and consequent dishonour (as he considered it) stared him in the face. His mind was so affected by his troubles that both his wife and daughter, towards the last, considered him to be hardly responsible for his own acts. In this state of desperation and misery, he – ' Here Mr Frank began to hesitate.

We have two ways in the law, of drawing evidence off nice and clear from an unwilling client or witness. We give him a fright or we treat him to a joke. I treated Mr Frank to a joke.

'Ah!' says I. 'I know what he did. He had a signature to write; and, by the most natural mistake in the world, he wrote another gentleman's name instead of his own – eh?'

'It was to a bill,' says Mr Frank, looking very crestfallen, instead of taking the joke. 'His principal creditor wouldn't wait till he could raise the money, or the greater part of it. But he was resolved, if he sold off everything, to get the amount and repay – '

'Of course!' says I. 'Drop that. The forgery was discovered. When?'

'Before even the first attempt was made to negotiate the bill. He had done the whole thing in the most absurdly and innocently wrong way. The person whose name he had used was a staunch friend of his, and a relation of his wife's: a good man as well as a rich one. He had influence with the chief creditor, and he used it nobly. He had a real affection for the unfortunate man's wife, and he proved it generously.'

'Come to the point,' says I. 'What did he do? In a business way, what did he do?'

'He put the false bill into the fire, drew a bill of his own to replace it, and then – only then – told my dear girl and her mother all that had happened. Can you imagine anything nobler?' asks Mr Frank.

'Speaking in my professional capacity, I can't imagine anything greener?' says I. 'Where was the father? Off, I suppose?'

'Ill in bed,' said Mr Frank, colouring. 'But, he mustered strength enough to write a contrite and grateful letter the same day, promising to prove himself worthy of the noble moderation and forgiveness extended to him, by selling off everything he possessed to repay his money debt. He did sell off everything, down to some old family pictures that were heirlooms; down to the little plate he had; down to the very tables and chairs that furnished his drawing room. Every farthing of the debt was paid; and he was left to begin the world again, with the kindest promises of help from the generous man who had forgiven him. It was too late. His crime of one rash moment – atoned for though it had been – preyed upon his mind. He became possessed with the idea that he had lowered himself forever in the estimation of his wife and daughter, and – '

'He died,' I cut in. 'Yes, yes, we know that. Let's go back for a minute to the contrite and grateful letter that he wrote. My experience in the law, Mr Frank, has convinced me that if everybody burnt everybody else's letters, half the Courts of Justice in this country might shut up shop. Do you happen to know whether the letter we are now speaking of contained anything like an avowal or confession of the forgery?'

'Of course it did,' says he. 'Could the writer express his contrition properly without making some such confession?'

'Quite easy, if he had been a lawyer,' says I. 'But never mind that; I'm going to make a guess, – a desperate guess, mind. Should I be altogether in error,' says I, 'if I thought that this letter had been stolen; and that the fingers of Mr Davager, of suspicious commercial celebrity, might possibly be the fingers which took it?' says I.

'That is exactly what I tried to make you understand,' cried Mr Frank.

'How did he communicate that interesting fact to you?'

'He has not ventured into my presence. The scoundrel actually had the audacity – '

'Aha!' says I. 'The young lady herself! Sharp practitioner, Mr Davager.'

'Early this morning, when she was walking alone in the shrubbery,' Mr Frank goes on, 'he had the assurance to approach her, and to say that he had been watching his opportunity of getting a private interview for days past. He then showed her – actually showed her – her unfortunate father's letter; put into her hands another letter directed to me; bowed, and walked off; leaving her half dead with astonishment and terror!'

'It was much better for you that you were not,' says I. 'Have you got that other letter?'

70

He handed it to me. It was so extremely humorous and short, that I remember every word of it at this distance of time. It began in this way:

To Francis Gatliffe, Esq., Jun. – Sir, – I have an extremely curious autograph letter to sell. The price is a Five hundred pound note. The young lady to whom you are to be married on Wednesday will inform you of the nature of the letter, and the genuineness of the autograph. If you refuse to deal, I shall send a copy to the local paper, and shall wait on your highly respected father with the original curiosity, on the afternoon of Tuesday next. Having come down here on family business, I have put up at the family hotel – being to be heard of at the Gatliffe Arms.

Your very obedient servant,
ALFRED DAVAGER.

'A clever fellow, that,' says I, putting the letter into my private drawer.

'Clever!' cries Mr Frank, 'he ought to be horsewhipped within an inch of his life. I would have done it myself, but she made me promise, before she told me a word of the matter, to come straight to you.'

'That was one of the wisest promises you ever made,' says I. 'We can't afford to bully this fellow, whatever else we may do with him. Don't think I am saying anything libellous against your excellent father's character when I assert that if he saw the letter he would certainly insist on your marriage being put off, at the very least?'

'Feeling as my father does about my marriage, he would insist on its being dropped altogether, if he saw this letter,' says Mr Frank, with a groan. 'But even that is not the worst of it.

The generous, noble girl herself says, that if the letter appears in the paper, with all the unanswerable comments this scoundrel would be sure to add to it, she would rather die than hold me to my engagement – even if my father would let me keep it.' He was a weak young fellow, and ridiculously fond of her. I brought him back to business with another rap of the paper-knife.

'Hold up, Mr Frank,' says I. 'I have a question or two more. Did you think of asking the young lady whether, to the best of her knowledge, this infernal letter was the only written evidence of the forgery now in existence?'

'Yes, I did think directly of asking her that,' says he; 'and she told me she was quite certain that there was no written evidence of the forgery, except that one letter.'

'Will you give Mr Davager his price for it?' says I.

'Yes,' says Mr Frank, as quick as lightning.

'Mr Frank,' says I, 'you came here to get my help and advice in this extremely ticklish business, and you are ready, as I know, without asking, to remunerate me for all and any of my services at the usual professional rate. Now, I've made up my mind to act boldly – desperately, if you like – on the hit or miss – win-all-or-lose-all principle – in dealing with this matter. Here is my proposal. I'm going to try if I can't do Mr Davager out of his letter. If I don't succeed before tomorrow afternoon, you hand him the money, and I charge you nothing for professional services. If I do succeed, I hand you the letter instead of Mr Davager; and you give me the money, instead of giving it to him. It's a precious risk for me, but I'm ready to run it. You must pay your five hundred any way. What do you say to my plan? Is it, Yes – Mr Frank – or, No?'

'Hang your questions!' cries Mr Frank, jumping up; 'you know it's Yes, ten thousand times over. Only you earn the money and – '

'And you will be too glad to give it to me. Very good. Now go home. Comfort the young lady – don't let Mr Davager so much as set eyes on you – keep quiet – leave everything to me – and feel as certain as you please that all the letters in the world can't stop your being married on Wednesday.' With these words I hustled him off out of the office; for I wanted to be left alone to make my mind up about what I should do.

The first thing, of course, was to have a look at the enemy. I wrote to Mr Davager, telling him that I was privately appointed to arrange the little business matter between himself and 'another party' (no names!) on friendly terms; and begging him to call on me at his earliest convenience. At the very beginning of the case, Mr Davager bothered me. His answer was that it would not be convenient to him to call till between six and seven in the evening. In this way, you see, he contrived to make me lose several precious hours, at a time when minutes almost were of importance. I had nothing for it, but to be patient, and to give certain instructions, before Mr Davager came, to my boy Tom.

There was never such a sharp boy of fourteen before, and there never will be again, as my boy, Tom. A spy to look after Mr Davager was, of course, the first requisite in a case of this kind; and Tom was the smallest, quickest, quietest, sharpest, stealthiest little snake of a chap that ever dogged a gentleman's steps and kept cleverly out of range of a gentleman's eyes. I settled it with the boy that he was not to show at all, when Mr Davager came; and that he was to wait to hear me ring the bell, when Mr Davager left. If I rang twice, he was to show the gentleman out. If I rang once, he was to keep out of the way and follow the gentleman wherever he went, till he got back to the inn. Those were the only preparations I could make to begin with; being obliged to wait, and let myself be guided by what turned up.

About a quarter to seven my gentleman came. In the profession of the law we get somehow quite remarkably mixed up with ugly people, blackguard people, and dirty people. But far away the ugliest and dirtiest blackguard I ever saw in my life was Mr Alfred Davager. He had greasy white hair and a mottled face. He was low in the forehead, fat in the stomach, hoarse in the voice, and weak in the legs. Both his eyes were bloodshot, and one was fixed in his head. He smelt of spirits, and carried a toothpick in his mouth. 'How are you? I've just done dinner,' says he – and he lights a cigar, sits down with his legs crossed, and winks at me.

I tried at first to take the measure of him in a wheedling, confidential way; but it was no good. I asked him in a facetious smiling manner, how he had got hold of the letter. He only told me in answer that he had been in the confidential employment of the writer of it, and that he had always been famous since infancy, for a sharp eye to his own interests. I paid him some compliments; but he was not to be flattered. I tried to make him lose his temper; but he kept it in spite of me. It ended in his driving me to my last resource – I made an attempt to frighten him.

'Before we say a word about the money,' I began, 'let me put a case, Mr Davager. The pull you have on Mr Francis Gatliffe is, that you can hinder his marriage on Wednesday. Now, suppose I have got a magistrate's warrant to apprehend you in my pocket? Suppose I have a constable to execute it in the next room? Suppose I bring you up tomorrow – the day before the marriage – charge you only generally with an attempt to extort money, and apply for a day's remand to complete the case? Suppose, as a suspicious stranger, you can't get bail in this town? Suppose – '

'Stop a bit,' says Mr Davager; 'Suppose I should not be the greenest fool that ever stood in shoes? Suppose I should not carry the letter about me? Suppose I should have given a certain envelope to a certain friend of mine in a certain place in this town? Suppose the letter should be inside that envelope, directed to old Gatliffe, side by side with a copy of the letter, directed to the editor of the local paper? Suppose my friend should be instructed to open the envelope, and take the letters to their right addressed, if I don't appear to claim them from him this evening? In short, my dear sir, suppose you were born yesterday, and suppose I wasn't?' – says Mr Davager, and winks at me again.

He didn't take me by surprise, for I never expected that he had the letter about him. I made a pretence of being very much taken aback, and of being quite ready to give in. We settled our business about delivering the letter and handing over the money, in no time. I was to draw out a document, which he was to sign. He knew the document was stuff and nonsense just as well as I did; and told me I was only proposing it to swell my client's bill. Sharp as he was, he was wrong there. The document was not to be drawn out to gain money from Mr Frank, but to gain time from Mr Davager. It served me as an excuse to put off the payment of the five hundred pounds till three o'clock on the Tuesday afternoon. The Tuesday morning Mr Davager said he should devote to his amusement, and asked me what sights were to be seen in the neighbourhood of the town. When I had told him, he pitched his toothpick into my grate – yawned – and went out.

I rang the bell once; waited till he had passed the window; and then looked after Tom. There was my jewel of a boy on the opposite side of the street, just setting his top going in the most playful manner possible. Mr Davager walked away up the street, towards the marketplace. Tom whipped his top up the street towards the marketplace too.

In a quarter of an hour he came back, with all his evidence collected in a beautifully clear and compact state. Mr Davager had walked to a public-house, just outside the town, in a lane leading to the high road. On a bench outside the public-house there sat a man smoking. He said 'All right?' and gave a letter to Mr Davager, who answered 'All right,' and walked back to the inn. In the hall he ordered hot rum and water, cigars, slippers, and a fire to be lit in his room. After that, he went upstairs, and Tom came away.

I now saw my road clear before me – not very far on, but still clear. I had housed the letter, in all probability for that night, at the Gatliffe Arms. After tipping Tom, I gave him directions to play about the door of the inn, and refresh himself, when he was tired, at the tart shop opposite – eating as much as he pleased, on the understanding that he crammed all the time with his eye on the window. If Mr Davager went out, or Mr Davager's friend called on him, Tom was to let me know. He was also to take a little note from me to the head chambermaid – an old friend of mine – asking her to step over to my office, on a private matter of business, as soon as her work was done for that night. After settling these little matters, having half an hour to spare, I turned to and did myself a bloater[56] at the office fire, and had a drop of gin and water hot, and felt comparatively happy.

When the head chambermaid came, it turned out, as good luck would have it, that Mr Davager had offended her. I no sooner mentioned him than she flew into a passion; and when I added, by way of clinching the matter, that I was retained to defend the interests of a very beautiful and deserving young lady (name not referred to, of course) against the most cruel underhand treachery on the part of Mr Davager, the head chambermaid was ready to go any lengths that she could safely to serve my cause. In few words, I discovered that Boots was to call Mr Davager at eight the next morning, and was to take his clothes downstairs to brush as usual. If Mr D. had not emptied his own pockets overnight, we arranged that Boots was to forget to empty them for him, and was to bring the clothes downstairs just as he found them. If Mr D.'s pockets were emptied, then, of course, it would be necessary to transfer the searching process to Mr D.'s room. Under any circumstances, I was certain of the head chambermaid; and under any circumstances also, the head chambermaid was certain of Boots.

I waited till Tom came home, looking very puffy and bilious about the face; but as to his intellects, if anything, rather sharper than ever. His report was uncommonly short and pleasant. The inn was shutting up; Mr Davager was going to bed in rather a drunken condition; Mr Davager's friend had never appeared. I sent Tom (properly instructed about keeping our man in view all the next morning) to his shake-down behind the office desk, where I heard him hiccupping half the night, as boys will, when over-excited and too full of tarts.

At half-past seven next morning, I slipped quietly into Boots's pantry. Down came the clothes. No pockets in trousers. Waistcoat pockets empty. Coat pockets with something in them. First, handkerchief; secondly, bunch of keys; thirdly, cigar case; fourthly, pocketbook. Of course I wasn't such a fool as to expect to find the letter there; but I opened the pocketbook with a certain curiosity, notwithstanding.

Nothing in the two pockets of the book but some old advertisements cut out of newspapers, a lock of hair tied round with a dirty bit of ribbon, a circular letter about a loan society, and some copies of verses not likely to suit any company that was not of an extremely wicked description. On the leaves of the pocketbook, people's addresses scrawled in pencil, and bets jotted down in red ink. On one leaf, by itself, this queer inscription: 'MEM. 5 ALONG. 4 ACROSS.' I understood everything but those words and figures; so of course I copied them out into my own book. Then I waited in the pantry, till Boots had brushed the clothes and had taken them upstairs. His report, when he came down was, that Mr D. had asked if it was a fine morning. Being told that it was, he had ordered breakfast at nine, and a saddle horse to be at the door at ten, to take him to Grimwith Abbey – one of the sights in our neighbourhood which I had told him of the evening before.

'I'll be here, coming in by the back way at half-past ten,' says I to the head chambermaid. 'To take the responsibility of making Mr Davager's bed off your hands for this morning only. I want to hire Sam for the morning. Put it down in the order-book that he's to be brought round to my office at ten.'

Sam was a pony, and I'd made up my mind that it would be beneficial to Tom's health, after the tarts, if he took a constitutional airing on a nice hard saddle in the direction of Grimwith Abbey.

'Anything else,' says the head chambermaid.

'Only one more favour,' says I. 'Would my boy Tom be very much in the way if he came, from now till ten, to help with the boots and shoes, and stood at his work close by this window which looks out on the staircase?'

'Not a bit,' says the head chambermaid.

'Thank you,' says I; and stepped back to my office directly.

When I had sent Tom off to help with the boots and shoes, I reviewed the whole case exactly as it stood at that time. There were three things Mr Davager might do with the letter.

He might give it to his friend again before ten – in which case, Tom would most likely see the said friend on the stairs. He might take it to his friend, or to some other friend, after ten – in which case, Tom was ready to follow him on Sam the pony. And, lastly, he might leave it hidden somewhere in the room at the inn – in which case, I was all ready for him with a search warrant of my own granting, under favour always of my friend the head chambermaid. So far I had my business arrangements all gathered up nice and compact in my own hands. Only two things bothered me: the terrible shortness of the time at my disposal, in case I failed in my first experiments for getting hold of the letter, and that queer inscription which I had copied out of the pocketbook.

'Mem. 5 Along. 4 Across.' It was the measurement, most likely, of something, and he was afraid of forgetting it; therefore, it was something important. Query – something about himself? Say '5' (inches) 'along' – he doesn't wear a wig. Say '5' (feet) 'along' – it can't be coat, waistcoat, trousers, or underclothing. Say '5' (yards) 'along' – it can't be anything about himself, unless he wears round his body the rope that he's sure to be hanged with one of these days. Then it is *not* something about himself. What do I know of that is important to him besides? I know of nothing but the Letter. Can the memorandum be connected with that? Say, yes. What do '5 along' and '4 across' mean then? The measurement of something he carries about with him? – or the measurement of something in his room? I could get pretty satisfactorily to myself as far as that; but I could get no further.

Tom came back to the office, and reported him mounted for his ride. His friend had never appeared. I sent the boy off, with his proper instructions, on Sam's back – wrote an encouraging letter to Mr Frank to keep him quiet – then slipped into the inn by the back way a little before half-past ten. The head chambermaid gave me a signal when the landing was clear. I got into his room without a soul but her seeing me, and locked the door immediately. The case was to a certain extent, simplified now. Either Mr Davager had ridden out with the letter about him, or he had left it in some safe hiding place in his room. I suspected it to be in his room, for a reason that will a little astonish you – his trunk, his dressing case, and all the drawers and cupboards were left open. I knew my customer, and I thought this extraordinary carelessness on his part rather suspicious.

Mr Davager had taken one of the best bedrooms at the Gatliffe Arms. Floor carpeted all over, walls beautifully papered, four-poster, and general furniture first-rate. I searched, to begin with, on the usual plan, examining every thing in every possible way, and taking more than an hour about it. No discovery. Then I pulled out a carpenter's rule which I had brought with me. Was there anything in the room which – either in inches, feet, or yards – answered to '5 along' and '4 across?' Nothing. I put the rule back in my pocket – measurement was no good evidently. Was there anything in the room that would count up to 5 one way and 4 another, seeing that nothing would measure up to it? I had got obstinately persuaded by this time that the letter must be in the room – principally because of the trouble I had had in looking after it. And persuading myself of that, I took it into my head next, just as obstinately, that '5 along' and '4 across' must be the right clue to find the letter by – principally because I hadn't left myself, after all my searching and thinking, even so much as the vestige of another guide to go by. '5 along' – where could I count five along the room, in any part of it?

Not on the paper. The pattern there was pillars of trellis-work and flowers, enclosing a plain green ground – only four pillars along the wall and only two across. The furniture? There were not five chairs, or five separate pieces of any furniture in the room altogether. The fringes that hung from the cornice of the bed? Plenty of them, at any rate! Up I jumped on the counterpane, with my penknife in my hand. Every way that '5 along' and '4 across' could be reckoned on those unlucky fringes, I reckoned on them – probed with my penknife – scratched with my nails – crunched with my fingers. No use; not a sign of a letter; and the time was getting on – oh, Lord! how the time did get on in Mr Davager's room that morning.

I jumped down from the bed, so desperate at my ill luck that I hardly cared whether anybody heard me or not. Quite a little cloud of dust rose at my feet as they thumped on the carpet. 'Hallo!' thought I; 'my friend the head chambermaid takes it easy here. Nice state for a carpet to be in, in one of the best bedrooms at the Gatliffe Arms.' Carpet! I had been jumping up on the bed, and staring up at the walls, but I had never so much as given a glance down at the carpet. Think of me pretending to be a lawyer, and not knowing how to look low enough!

The carpet! It had been a stout article in its time; had evidently begun in a drawing room; then descended to a coffee room; then gone upstairs altogether to a bedroom. The ground was brown, and the pattern was bunches of leaves and roses speckled over the ground at regular distances. I reckoned up the bunches. Ten along the room – eight across it. When I had stepped out five one way and four the other, and was down on my knees on the centre bunch, as true as I sit on this bench, I could hear my own heart beating so loud that it quite frightened me.

I looked narrowly all over the bunch, and I felt all over it with the ends of my fingers; and nothing came of that. Then I scraped it over slowly and gently with my nails. My second fingernail stuck a little at one place. I parted the pile of the carpet over that place, and saw a thin slit, which had been hidden by the pile being smoothed over it – a slit about half an inch long, with a little end of brown thread, exactly the colour of the carpet-ground, sticking out about a quarter of an inch from the middle of it. Just as I laid hold of the thread gently, I heard a footstep outside the door.

It was only the head chambermaid. 'Havn't you done yet?' she whispers.

'Give me two minutes,' says I; 'and don't let anybody come near the door – whatever you do, don't let anybody startle me again by coming near the door.'

I took a little pull at the thread, and heard something rustle. I took a longer pull, and out came a piece of paper, rolled up tight like those candle-lighters that the ladies make. I unrolled it – and, by George! gentlemen all, there was the letter!

The original letter! – I knew it by the colour of the ink. The letter that was worth five hundred pound to me! It was all I could do to keep myself at first from throwing my hat into the air, and hooraying like mad. I had to take a chair and sit quiet in it for a minute or two, before I could cool myself down to my proper business level. I knew that I was safely down again when I found myself pondering how to let Mr Davager know that he had been done by the innocent country attorney, after all.

It was not long before a nice little irritating plan occurred to me. I tore a blank leaf out of my pocketbook, wrote on it with my pencil 'Change for a five hundred pound note,' folded up the paper, tied the thread to it, poked it back into the hiding place, smoothed over the pile of the carpet, and – as everybody in this place guesses before I can tell them – bolted off to Mr Frank. He, in his turn, bolted off to show the letter to the young lady, who first certified to its genuineness, then dropped it into the fire, and then took the initiative for the first time since her marriage engagement, by flinging her arms round his neck, kissing him with all her might, and going into hysterics in his arms. So at least Mr Frank told me; but that's not evidence. It is evidence, however, that I saw them married with my own eyes on the Wednesday; and that while they went off in a carriage and four to spend the honeymoon, I went off on my own legs to open a credit at the Town and County Bank with a five hundred pound note in my pocket.

As to Mr Davager, I can tell you nothing about him, except what is derived from hearsay evidence, which is always unsatisfactory evidence, even in a lawyer's mouth.

My boy, Tom, although twice kicked off by Sam the pony, never lost hold of the bridle, and kept his man in sight from first to last. He had nothing particular to report, except that on the way out to the Abbey Mr Davager had stopped at the public-house, had spoken a word or two to his friend of the night before, and had handed him what looked like a bit of paper. This was no doubt a clue to the thread that held the letter, to be used in case of accidents. In every other respect Mr D. had ridden out and ridden in like an ordinary sightseer. Tom reported him to me as having dismounted at the hotel about two. At half-past, I locked my office door, nailed a card under the knocker with 'not at home till tomorrow' written on it, and retired to a friend's house a mile or so out of the town for the rest of the day.

Mr Davager left the Gatliffe Arms that night, with his best clothes on his back, and with all the valuable contents of his dressing case in his pockets. I am not in a condition to state whether he ever went through the form of asking for his bill or not; but I can positively testify that he never paid it, and that the effects left in his bedroom did not pay it either. When I add to these fragments of evidence, that he and I have never met (luckily for me), since I jockeyed him out of his bank note, I have about fulfilled my implied contract as maker of a statement, with the present company as hearers of a statement.

THE FIFTH POOR TRAVELLER
[by George A. Sala]

Do you know – the journeyman watchmaker from Geneva began – do you know those long straight lines of French country, over which I have often walked? Do you know those rivers so long, so uniform in breadth, so dully gray in hue, that in despair at their regularity, you momentarily libel nature as being only a grand canal commissioner after all? Do you know the long funereal rows of poplars, or dreary parallelograms of osiers,[57] that fringe those river banks; the long white roads, hedgeless, but, oh! so dismally ditchful; the long, low stone walls; the long farmhouses, without a spark of the robust, leafy, cheerful life of the English homesteads; the long fields, scarcely evergreen, but of an ashen tone, wearily furrowed, as though the earth had grown old and was beginning to show the crow's feet; the long, interminable gray French landscape? The sky itself seems longer than it ought to be; and the clouds stretch away to goodness knows where in long low banks, as if the heavens had been ruled with a parallel. If a vehicle passes you it is only a wofully long diligence, lengthened yellow ugliness long drawn out, with a seemingly endless team of horses, and a long, stifling cloud of dust behind it; a driver for the wheelers with a whip seven times as long as it ought to be; and a postilion for the leaders with boots long enough for seven-leaguers.[58] His oaths are long; the horses' manes are long; their tails are so long that they are obliged to have them tied up with straw. The stages are long, the journey long, the fares long – the whole longitudinal carriage leaves a long melancholy jingle of bells behind it.

Yes: French scenery is very lengthy; so I settled in my mind at least, as I walked with long strides along the white French road. A longer me – my shadow – walked before me, bending its back and drooping its arms, and angularising its elongated legs like drowsy compasses. The shadow looked tired: I felt so. I had been oppressed by length all day. I had passed a long procession – some hundreds of boys in gray great coats and red trousers: soldiers. I had found their guns and bayonets too long, their coats disproportionately lengthy; the moustaches of their officers ridiculously elongated. There was no end of them – their rolling drums, baggage waggons, and led horses. I had passed a team of bullocks ploughing: they looked as long as the lane that hath no turning. A long man followed them smoking a long pipe. A wretched pig I saw, too – a long, lean, bristly, lanky-legged monstrosity, without even a curly tail, for his tail was long and pendent; a miserable pig, half-snouted greyhound, half-abashed weazel, whole hog, and an eyesore to me. I was a long way from home. I had the spleen.[59] I wanted something short – not to drink, but a short break in the long landscape, a house, a knoll, a clump of trees – anything to relieve this long purgatory.

Whenever I feel inclined to take a more than ordinarily dismal view of things, I find it expedient to take a pipe of tobacco instead. As I wanted to rest, however, as well as smoke, I had to walk another long mile. When I descried a house, in front thereof was a huge felled tree, and on the tree I sat and lighted my pipe. The day was of no particular character whatever: neither wet nor dry, cold nor hot – neither springy, summery, autumnal, nor wintry.

The house I was sitting opposite to, might have been one of public entertainment (for it was a cabaret) if there had been any public in the neighbourhood to be entertained, which (myself excepted) I considered doubtful. It seemed to me as if Bacchus, roving about on the loose, had dropped a stray tub here on the solitary road, and no longer coming that way, the tub itself had gone to decay – had become unhooped, mouldy, leaky. I declare that, saving a certain fanciful resemblance to the barrel on which the god of wine is generally supposed to take horse exercise, the house had no more shape than a lump of cheese that one might dig hap-hazard from a soft, double Gloucester. The windows were patches and the doorway had evidently been made subsequently to the erection of the building, and looked like an excrescence as it was. The top of the house had been pelted with mud, thatch, tiles, and slates, rather than roofed; and a top room jutted out laterally from one of the walls, supported beneath by crazy uprights, like a poor relation clinging to a genteel kinsman nearly as poor. The walls had been plastered once, but the plaster had peeled off in places, and mud and wattles[60] peeped through like a beggar's bare knee through his torn trousers. An anomalous wooden ruin, that might have been a barrel in the beginning, then a dog kennel, then a dustbin, then a hen coop, seemed fast approximating (eked out by some rotten palings and half a deal box[61]) to a pigstye: perhaps my enemy the long pig with the pendent tail lived there when he was at home. A lively old birch broom, senile but twiggy, thriving under a kindly manure of broken bottles and woodashes, was the only apology for trees, hedges, or vegetation generally, visible. If wood was deficient, however, there was plenty of water. Behind the house, where it had been apparently raining for some years, a highly respectable puddle, as far as mud and stagnation went, had formed, and, on the surface of it drifted a solitary, purposeless, soleless old shoe, and one dismal duck which no amount of green peas would have ever persuaded me to eat. There was a chimney to the house, but not in the proper place, of course: it came out of one of the walls, close to the impromptu pigstye, in the shape of a rusty, battered iron funnel. There had never been anything to speak of done in the way of painting to the house; only some erratic journeyman painter passing that way had tried his brushes in red, green, and yellow smudges on the wall; had commenced dead colouring one of the window sills; and had then given it up as a bad job. Some pretentious announcements relative to 'Good wines and liquors;' and '*Il y a un billard*'[62] there had been once above the door, but the rain had washed out some of the letters, and the smoke had obscured others, and the plaster had peeled off from beneath more; and some, perhaps, the writer had never finished; so the inscriptions were a mere wandering piece of idiotcy now. If anything were wanted to complete the general wretchedness of this house of dismal appearances it would have been found in the presence of a ghostly set of ninepins that Rip Van Winkle might have played with.[63]

All these things were not calculated to inspire cheerfulness. I continued smoking, however, and thought that by and by I would enter the cabaret, and see if there were any live people there; which appeared unlikely.

All at once, there came out to me from the house a little man. It is not at all derogating from his manhood to state that he was also a little boy, of perhaps eight years old; but in look, in eye, in weird fur-cap, in pea-coat, blue canvas trousers, and sabots,[64] he was at least thirty-seven years of age. He had a remarkable way, too, of stroking his chin with his hand. He looked at me long and fully, but without the slightest rudeness, or intrusive curiosity; then sitting by my side on the great felled tree he smoked a mental pipe (so it appeared to me) while I smoked a material one. Once, I think, he softly felt the texture of my coat; but I did not turn my head, and pretended not to notice.

We were getting on thus, very sociably together, without saying a word, when, having finished my pipe I replaced it in my pouch, and began to remove a little of the superfluous dust from my boots. My pulverous appearance was the cue for the little man to address himself to speech.

'I see,' said he, gravely, 'you are one of those poor travellers whom mamma tells us we are to take such care of. Attend, attend, I will do your affair for you in a moment.'

He trotted across to the cabaret, and after a lapse of two or three minutes returned with a tremendous hunch of bread, a cube of cheese – which smelt, as the Americans say, rather loud, but was excellently well-tasted – and an anomalous sort of vessel that was neither a jug, a mug, a cup, a glass, nor a pint-pot, but partook of the characteristics of all – full of Macon wine.[65]

'This is Friday,' added the little man, 'and meagre day, else should you be regaled with sausage – and of Lyons[66] – of which we have as long as that;' saying which he extended his little arms to perhaps half a yard's distance one from the other.

I did not care to inform the little man that I was of a persuasion that did not forbid the eating of sausages on Fridays. I ate the bread and cheese and drank the wine, all of which were very good and very palatable, very contentedly: the little man sitting by, the while, nursing one of his short legs, and talking to himself softly.

When I had finished I lighted another pipe, and went in for conversation with the little man. We soon exhausted the ordinary topics of conversation, such as the weather, the distance from the last town, and the distance to the next. I found that the little man's forte was interrogatory, and let him have his swing that way.

'You come from a long way?' he asked.

'A long way,' I answered. 'From beyond the Sous-prefecture, beyond Nantes, beyond Brest and L'Orient.'

'But from a town, always? You come from a town where there are a great many people, and where they make wheels?'

I answered that I came from a large town, and that I had no doubt, though I had no personal experience in the matter, that wheels were made there.

'And cannot you make wheels?'

I told him I was not a wheelwright; I only made the wheels of watches, which were not the wheels he meant.

'Because,' the little man went on to say, softly, and more to himself than to me, 'mamma said he liked more to live in towns, where there were many people, and M. le Curé said that wherever wheels were made he could gain his bread.'

I could not make much of this statement, so I puffed away at my pipe, and listened.

'By the way,' my small but elderly companion remarked, 'would you have any objection to my bringing my sister to you?'

The more I saw of so original a family the better, I thought; so I told him I should be delighted to see his sister.

He crossed over to the cabaret again, and almost immediately afterwards returned, leading a little maid.

She seemed about a year younger, or a year older than her brother. I could not tell which. It did not matter which. She was very fair, and her auburn locks were confined beneath a little prim blue cap. Mittens, a striped woollen shirt, a smart white chemisette, blue hose, and trim little sabots, all these had the little maid. She had a little chain and golden cross; a pair of scissors hanging by a string to her girdle, a black tabinet[67] apron, and a little silver ring on the forefinger of her left hand. Her eyes were very blue, but they could not see my dusty boots, my pipe, and three days' beard. They could not see the great felled tree, her brother in his pea-coat, the sky, the sun going down beyond the long straight banks of trees. They had never seen any of these things. The little maid was blind.

She had known all about me, however, as far as the boots, the pipe, the dust, the bread and cheese, my having come a long way, and not being a wheelwright went, long since. At least, she seemed quite au fait on general topics connected with my social standing, or rather sitting, on the tree: and taking a seat on one side of me: her brother, the little man, on the other, the two little children began to chatter most delightfully.

Mamma worked in the fields. In her own fields. She had three fields. Fields large as that (distance measured by little maid's arms after the manner of her brother in reference to the sausage question). Papa made wheels. They loved him very much, but he beat mamma, and drank wine by cannons. When he was between two wines (that is, drunk), he knocked Lili's head against the wall (Lili was the little man). When M. le Curé tried to bring him to a sense of the moral, he laughed at his nose. He was a farcer was Papa. He made beautiful wheels, and earned money like that (arm measurement again), except when he went weddingising (*nocer*)[68], when he always came back between two wines, and between the two fell to the ground. Papa went away, a long time, a very long time ago. Before the white calf at the farm was born. Before André drew the bad number in the conscription, and went away to Africa. Before Lili had his grand malady (little man looked a hundred years old with the conscious experience of a grand malady. What was it? Elephantiasis, spasmodic neuralgia?[69] Something wonderful, with a long name, I am sure). Papa sold the brown horse, and the great bed in oak, before he went away. He also *briséd* Mamma's head with a bottle, previous to his departure. He was coming back some day. He was sure to come back. M. le Curé said no, and that he was a worth nothing, but mamma said, Yes, and cried; 'though for *my* part,' concluded the little maid, when between herself and brother she had told me all this, '*I* think that poor papa never will come back, but he has gone away among those Bedouin Turks, who are so *méchants*,[70] and that they have eaten him up.'

The little blind fairy made this statement with an air of such positive yet mild conviction, crossing her mites of hands in her lap as she did so, that for the moment I would have no more attempted to question the prevalence of cannibalism in Constantinople than to deny the existence of the setting sun.

While these odd little people were thus entertaining me, Heaven knows where my thoughts were wandering. This strange life they led. The mother away at work; the drunken wheelwright father a fugitive (he must have been an awful ruffian); and, strangest of all strange phases, that these two little ones should be left to keep a public-house! I thought of all these things, and then my thoughts came back to, and centred themselves in the weird little figure of the blind girl beside me. It was but a poor little blind girl in a blue petticoat and sabots; yet so exquisitely regular were the features, so golden the hair, so firm and smooth, and white – not marble, not wax, not ivory, yet partaking of all three the complexion, so symmetrical every line, and so gloriously harmonious the whole combination of lines, that the little maid might have been taken then and there as she sat, popped in a frame, with 'Raffaelle pinxit,'[71] in the corner, and purchased on the nail for five thousand guineas.

I could not help noticing from time to time, during our conversation, that the little man in the pea-coat turned aside to whisper somewhat mysteriously to his sister, and then looked at me more mysteriously still. He appeared to have something on his mind, and after a nod of apparent acquiescence on the part of the little blind girl, it soon came out what the something was.

'My sister and I,' said this small person, 'hope that you will not be offended with us, but would you have any objection to show us your tongue?'

This was, emphatically, a startler. Could the little man be a physician as well as a publican? I did as he asked me; though I am afraid I looked very foolish, and shut my eyes as I thrust forth the member he desired to inspect. He appeared highly gratified with the sight of my tongue, communicating the results of his observation thereof to his sister, who clapped her hands, and seemed much pleased. Then he condescended to explain.

'You see,' said he, 'that you told us you came from a distant country; that is well seen, for though you speak French like a little sheep, you do not speak it with the same tongue that we do.'

My experience of the court-martial scene in *Black-Eyed Susan*,[72] had taught me that it was possible to play the fiddle like an angel, but this was the first time I had ever heard of a grown man talking like a little sheep. I took it as a compliment, however (whether I was right or wrong in doing so is questionable), and waited to hear more.

'And my sister says that the reason why all strangers from far countries cannot speak as we do, is, because they have a dark line right down their tongues. Now you must have a line down your tongue, though I am not tall enough to see it!'

The creed of this valiant little fellow in respect to lines and tongues had evidently been built, long since, upon a rock of ages of loving faith in what his sister had told him. Besides, how do *I* know? *I* never saw my tongue except in a looking-glass, and that may have been false. My tongue may have five hundred lines crossing it at every imaginable angle, for aught I know.

So, we three, oddly assorted trio went chattering on, till the shadows warned me that twilight was fast approaching, and that I had two miles to walk to the town where I had appointed to sleep. Remembering then, that the little man had 'done my affair for me,' in an early stage of our interview in the way of bread and cheese and wine, and not choosing to be really the poor traveller I seemed, I drew out a five-franc piece, and proffered payment.

Both the children refused the coin; and the little maid said gravely, 'Mamma said that we were always to take care of poor travellers. What we have given you is *pour l'amour de Dieu*, – for God's sake.'

I tried to force some trifle on them as a gift, but they would have none of my coin. Seeing then that I looked somewhat disappointed, the little man, like a profound diplomatist as he was, smoothed away the difficulty in a moment.

'If you like to go as far as you can see to the right, towards the town,' he said, 'you will find a blind old woman, playing upon a flageolet,[73] and sitting at a cakestall by the way side. And if you like to buy us some gingerbread: – for three sous she will give you – oh! like that!' For the last time in this history he extended his arms in sign of measurement.

I went as far as I could see, which was not far, and found the blind old woman playing on a flageolet, and not seeing at all. Of her, did I purchase gingerbread, with brave white almonds in it: following my own notions of measurement, I may hint, in respect to the number of sous-worth.

Bringing it back to the children, I took them up, and kissed them and bade them good-bye. Then I left them to the ginger-bread and the desolate cabaret, until mamma should return from the fields, and that famous domestic institution, the '*soupe*,' of which frequent mention had already been made during our intercourse, should be ready.

I have never seen them since; I shall never see them again; but, if it ever be my lot to be no longer solitary, I pray that I may have a boy and girl, as wise, and good, and innocent as I am sure those little children were.

THE SIXTH POOR TRAVELLER
[by Eliza Lynn Linton]

Was the little widow. She had been sitting by herself in the darkest corner of the room all this time; her pale face often turned anxiously toward the door, and her hollow eyes watching restlessly, as if she expected someone to appear. She was very quiet, very grateful for any little kindness, very meek in the midst of her wildness. There was a strained expression in her eyes, and a certain excited air about her altogether, that was very near insanity; it seemed as if she had once been terrified by some sudden shock, to the verge of madness.

When her turn came to speak, she began in a low voice – her eyes still glancing to the door – and spoke as if to herself rather than to the rest of us; speaking low but rapidly – somewhat like a somnambule repeating a lesson:

They advised me not to marry him (she began). They told me he was wild – unprincipled – bad; but I did not care for what they said. I loved him and I disbelieved them. I never thought about his goodness – I only knew that he was beautiful and gifted beyond all that I had ever met within our narrow society. I loved him, with no passing schoolgirl fancy, but with my whole heart – my whole soul. I had no life, no joy, no hope without him, and heaven would have been no heaven to me if he had not been there. I say all this, simply to show what a madness of devotion mine was.

My dear mother was very kind to me throughout. She had loved my father, I believe, almost to the same extent; so that she could sympathise with me even while discouraging. She told me that I was wrong and foolish, and that I should repent: but I kissed away the painful lines between her eyes, and made her smile when I tried to prove to her that love was better than prudence. So we married: not so much without the consent as against the wish of my family; and even that wish withheld in sorrow and in love. I remember all this now, and see the true proportions of everything; then, I was blinded by my passions, and understood nothing.

We went away to our pretty, bright home in one of the neighbourhoods of London, near a park. We lived there for many months – I in a state of intoxication rather than of earthly happiness, and he was happy, too, then, for I am sure he was innocent, and I know he loved me. Oh, dreams – dreams!

I did not know my husband's profession. He was always busy and often absent; but he never told me what he did. There had been no settlements either, when I married. He said he had a conscientious scruple against them; that they were insulting to a man's honour and degrading to any husband. This was one of the reasons why, at home, they did not wish me to marry him. But I was only glad to be able to show him how I trusted him, by meeting his wishes and refusing, on my own account, to accept the legal protection of settlements. It was such a pride to me to sacrifice all to him. Thus I knew nothing of his real life – his pursuits or his fortunes. I never asked him any questions, as much from indifference to everything but his love as from a wifely blindness of trust. When he came home at night, sometimes very gay, singing opera songs, and calling me his little Medora,[74] as he used when in a good humour, I was gay too, and grateful. And when he came home moody and irritable – which he used to do, often, after we had been married about three months, once even threatening to strike me, with that fearful glare in his eyes I remember so well, and used to see so often afterwards – then I was patient and silent, and never attempted even to take his hand or kiss his forehead when he bade me be still and not interrupt him. He was my law, and his approbation the sunshine of my life; so that my very obedience was selfishness; for my only joy was to see him happy, and my only duty to obey him.

My sister came to visit us. My husband had seen very little of her before our marriage; for she had often been from home when he was with us, down at Hurst Farm – that was the name of my dear mother's place – and I had always fancied they had not liked even the little they had seen of each other. Ellen was never loud or importunate in her opposition. I knew that she did not like the marriage, but she did not interfere. I remember quite well the only time she spoke openly to me on the subject how she flung herself at my knees, with a passion very rare in her, beseeching me to pause and reflect, as if I had sold myself to my ruin when I promised to be Harry's wife. How she prayed! Poor Ellen! I can see her now, with her heavy, uncurled hair falling on her neck as she knelt half undressed, her large eyes full of agony and supplication, like a martyred saint praying. Poor Ellen! I thought her prejudiced then; and this unspoken injustice has lain like a heavy crime on my heart ever since: for I know that I judged her wrongfully, and that I was ungrateful for her love.

She came to see us. This was about a year and a half after I married. She was more beautiful than ever, but somewhat sterner, as well as sadder. She was tall, strong in person, and dignified in manner. There was a certain manly character in her beauty, as well as in her mind, that made one respect and fear her too a little. I do not mean that she was masculine, or hard, or coarse: she was a true woman in grace and gentleness; but she was braver than women in general. She had more self-reliance, was more resolute and steadfast, and infinitely less impulsive, and was more active and powerful in body.

My husband was very kind to her. He paid her great attention; and sometimes I half perceived that he liked her almost better than he liked me – he used to look at her so often: but with such a strange expression in his eyes! I never could quite make it out, whether it was love or hate. Certainly, after she came his manner changed towards me. I was not jealous. I did not suspect this change from any small feeling of wounded self-love, or from any envy of my sister; but I saw it – I felt it in my heart – yet without connecting it with Ellen in any way. I knew that he no longer loved me as he used to do, but I did not think he loved her; at least, not with the same kind of love. I used to be surprised at Ellen's conduct to him. She was more than cold; she was passionately rude and unkind; not so much when I was there as when I was away. For I used to hear her voice speaking in those deep indignant tones that are worse to bear than the harshest scream of passion; and sometimes I used to hear hard words – he speaking at the first soft and pleadingly, often to end in a terrible burst of anger and imprecation. I could not understand why they quarrelled. There was a mystery between them that I did not know of; and I did not like to ask them, for I was afraid of them both – as much afraid of Ellen as of my husband – and I felt like a reed between them – as if I should have been crushed beneath any storm I might chance to wake up. So, I was silent – suffering alone, and bearing a cheerful face so far as I could.

Ellen wanted me to return home with her. Soon after she came, and soon after I heard the first dispute between them, she urged me to go back to Hurst Farm; at once, and for a long time. Weak as I am by nature, it has always been a marvel to me since, how strong I was where my love for my husband was concerned. It seemed impossible for me to yield to any pressure against him. I believe now that a very angel could not have turned me from him!

At last she said to me in a low voice: 'Mary, this is madness! – it is almost sinful! Can you not see – can you not hear?' And then she stopped and would say no more, though I urged her to tell me what she meant. For this terrible mystery began to weigh on me painfully, and, for all that I trembled so much to fathom it, I had begun to feel that any truth would be better than such a life of dread. I seemed to be living among shadows; my very husband and sister not real, for their real lives were hidden from me. But I was too timid to insist on an explanation, and so things went on in their old way.

In one respect only, changing still more painfully, still more markedly; in my husband's conduct to me. He was like another creature altogether to me now, he was so altered. He seldom spoke to me at all, and he never spoke kindly. All that I did annoyed him, all that I said irritated him; and once (the little widow covered her face with her hands and shuddered) he spurned me with his foot and cursed me, one night in our own room, when I knelt weeping before him, supplicating him for pity's sake to tell me how I had offended him. But I said to myself that he was tired, annoyed, and that it was irritating to see a loving woman's tears; and so I excused him, as oftentimes before, and went on loving him all the same – God forgive me for my idolatry!

Things had been very bad of late between Ellen and my husband. But the character of their discord was changed. Instead of reproaching, they watched each other incessantly. They put me in mind of fencers – my husband on the defensive.

'Mary,' said my sister to me suddenly, coming to the sofa where I was sitting embroidering my poor baby's cap. 'What does your Harry do in life? What is his profession?'

She fixed her eyes on me earnestly.

'I do not know, darling,' I answered, vaguely. 'He has no profession that I know of.'

'But what fortune has he, then? Did he not tell you what his income was, and how obtained, when he married? To us, he said only that he had so much a year – a thousand a year; and he would say no more. But, has he not been more explicit with you?'

'No,' I answered, considering; for, indeed, I had never thought of this. I had trusted so blindly to him in everything that it would have seemed to me, a profound insult to have even asked of his affairs. 'No, he never told me anything about his fortune, Ellen. He gives me money when I want it, and is always generous. He seems to have plenty; whenever it is asked for, he has it by him, and gives me even more than I require.'

Still her eyes kept looking at me in that strange manner. 'And this is all you know?'

'Yes – all. What more should I wish to know? Is he not the husband, and has he not absolute right over everything! I have no business to interfere.' The words sound harsher now than they did then, for I spoke lovingly.

Ellen touched the little cap I held. 'Does not this make you anxious?' she said. 'Can you not fear as a mother, even while you love as a wife?'

'Fear, darling! Why? What should I fear, or whom? What is there, Ellen, on your heart?' I then added passionately. 'Tell me at once; for I know that you have some terrible secret concealed from me; and I would rather know anything – whatever it may be – than live on, longer, in this kind of suspense and anguish! It is too much for me to bear, Ellen.'

She took my hands. 'Have you strength?' she said, earnestly. 'Could you really bear the truth?' Then seeing my distress, for

I had fallen into a kind of hysterical fit – I was very delicate then – she shook her head in despair, and, letting my hands fall heavily on my lap, said in an undertone, 'No, no! she is too weak – too childish!' Then she went upstairs abruptly; and I heard her walking about her own room for nearly an hour after, in long steady steps.

I have often thought that, had she told me then, and taken me to her heart – her strong, brave, noble heart – I could have derived courage from it, and could have borne the dreadful truth I was forced to know afterwards. But the strong are so impatient with us! They leave us too soon – their own strength revolts at our weakness; so we are often left, broken in this weakness, for want of a little patience and sympathy.

Harry came in, a short time after Ellen had left me. 'What has she been saying?' he cried, passionately. His eyes were wild and bloodshot; his beautiful black hair flung all in disorder about his face.

'Dear Harry, she has said nothing about you,' I answered, trembling. 'She only asked what was your profession, and how much we had a year. That was all.'

'Why did she ask this? What business was it of hers?' cried Harry, fiercely. 'Tell me;' and he shook me roughly, 'what did you answer her, little fool?'

'Oh, nothing;' and I began to cry: it was because he frightened me. 'I said, what is true, that I knew nothing of your affairs, as indeed what concern is it of mine? I could say nothing more, Harry.'

'Better that than too much,' he muttered; and then he flung me harshly back on the sofa, saying, 'Tears and folly and weakness! The same round – always the same! Why did I marry a mere pretty doll – a plaything – no wife!'

And then he seemed to think he had said too much: for he came to me and kissed me, and said that he loved me. But, for the first time in our married life his kisses did not soothe me, nor did I believe his assurances.

All that night I heard Ellen walk steadily and unresting through her room. She never slackened her pace, she never stopped, she never hurried; but, the same slow measured tread went on; the firm foot, yet light, falling as if to music, her very step the same mixture of manliness and womanhood as her character.

After this burst of passion Harry's tenderness to me became unbounded; as if he wished to make up to me for some wrong. I need not say how soon I forgave him, nor how much I loved him again. All my love came back in one full boundless tide; and the current of my being set towards him again as before. If he had asked me for my life then, as his mere fancy, to destroy, I would have given it him. I would have lain down and died, if he had wished to see the flowers grow over my grave.

My husband and Ellen grew more estranged as his affection seemed to return to me. His manner to her was defying; hers to him comtemptuous. I heard her call him villain once, in the garden below the windows; at which he laughed – his wicked laugh, and said 'tell her, and see if she will believe you!'

I was sitting in the window, working. It was a cold damp day in the late autumn, when those chill fogs of November are just beginning; those fogs with the frost in them, that steal into one's very heart. It was a day when a visible blight is in the air, when death is abroad everywhere, and suffering and crime. I was alone in the drawing room. Ellen was upstairs, and my husband, as I believed, in the City. But

I have remembered since, that I heard the hall door softly opened, and a footstep steal quietly by the drawing room up the stairs. The evening was just beginning to close in – dull, gray, and ghostlike; the dying daylight melting into the long shadows that stalked like wandering ghosts about the fresh-made grave of nature. I sat working still, at some of those small garments about which I dreamed such fond dreams, and wove such large hopes of happiness; and as I sat, while the evening fell heavy about me, a mysterious shadow of evil passed over me, a dread presentiment, a consciousness of ill, that made me tremble, as if in ague[75] – angry at myself though for my folly. But, it was reality. It was no hysterical sinking of the spirits that I felt; no mere nervousness or cowardice; it was something I had never known before; a knowledge, a presence, a power, a warning word, a spirit's cry, that had swept by me as the fearful evil marched on to its conclusion.

I heard a faint scream upstairs. It was so faint I could scarcely distinguish it from a sudden rush of wind through an opening door, or the chirp of a mouse behind the wainscot. Presently, I heard the same sound again; and then a dull muffled noise overhead, as of someone walking heavily, or dragging a heavy weight across the floor. I sat petrified by fear. A nameless agony was upon me that deprived me of all power of action. I thought of Harry and I thought of Ellen, in an inextricable cypher of misery and agony; but I could not have defined a line in my own mind; I could not have explained what it was I feared. I only knew that it was sorrow that was to come, and sin. I listened, but all was still again; once only, I thought I heard a low moan, and once a muttering voice – which I know now to have been my husband's, speaking passionately to himself.

And then his voice swept stormfully through the house, crying wildly, 'Mary, Mary! Quick here! Your sister! Ellen!'

I ran upstairs. It seems to me now, that I almost flew. I found Ellen lying on the floor of her own room, just inside the door; her feet towards the door of my husband's study, which was immediately opposite her room. She was fainting; at least I thought so then. We raised her up between us; my husband trembling more than I; and I unfastened her gown, and threw water on her face, and pushed back her hair; but she did not revive. I told Harry to go for a doctor. A horrid thought was stealing over me; but he lingered, as I fancied, unaccountably and cruelly, though I twice asked him to go. Then, I thought that perhaps he was too much overcome; so I went to him, and kissed him, and said, 'She will soon be better, Harry,' cheerfully, to cheer him. But I felt in my heart that she was no more.

At last, after many urgent entreaties, and after the servants had come up, clustering in a frightened way round the bed – but he sent them away again immediately – he put on his hat, and went out, soon returning with a strange man; not our own doctor. This man was rude and coarse, and ordered me aside, as I stood bathing my sister's face, and pulled her arm and hand roughly, to see how dead they fell, and stooped down close to her lips – I thought he touched them even – all in a violent and insolent way, that shocked me and bewildered me. My husband stood in the shadow, ghastly pale, but not interfering.

It was too true, what the strange man had said so coarsely. She was dead. Yes; the creature that an hour ago had been so full of life, so beautiful, so resolute, and young, was now a stiffening corpse, inanimate and dead, without life and without hope. Oh! that word had set my brain on fire! Dead!

here, in my house, under my roof – dead so mysteriously, so strangely – why? How? It was a fearful dream, it was no truth that lay there. I was in a nightmare; I was not sane; and thinking how ghastly it all was, I fainted softly on the bed, no one knowing, till some time after, that I had fallen, and was not praying. When I recovered I was in my own room, alone. Crawling feebly to my sister's door, I found that she had been washed and dressed, and was now laid out on her bed. It struck me that all had been done in strange haste; Harry telling me the servants had done it while I fainted. I knew afterwards that he had told them it was I, and that I would have no help. The mystery of it all was soon to be unravelled.

One thing I was decided on – to watch by my sister this night. It was in vain that my husband opposed me; in vain that he coaxed me by his caresses, or tried to terrify me with angry threats. Something of my sister's nature seemed to have passed into me; and unless he had positively prevented me by force, no other means would have had any effect. He gave way to me at last – angrily – and the night came on and found me sitting by the bedside watching my dear sister.

How beautiful she looked! Her face, still with the gentle mark of sorrow on it that it had in life, looked so grand! She was so great, so pure; she was like a goddess sleeping; she was not like a mere woman of this earth. She did not seem to be dead; there was life about her yet, for there was still the look of power and of human sympathy that she used to have when alive. The soul was there still, and love, and knowledge.

By degrees a strange feeling of her living presence in the room came over me. Alone in the still midnight, with no sound, no person near me, it seemed as if I had leisure and power to pass into the world beyond the grave. I felt my sister near me; I felt the passing of her life about me, as when one sleeps, but still is conscious that another life is weaving in with ours. It seemed as if her breath fell warm on my face; as if her shadowy arms held me in their clasp; as if her eyes were looking through the darkness at me; as if I held her hands in mine, and her long hair floated round my forehead. And then, to shake off these fancies, and convince myself that she was really dead, I looked again and again at her lying there: a marble corpse, ice-cold with the lips set and rigid, and the death band[76] beneath her chin. There she was, stiff in her white shroud, the snowy linen pressing so lightly on her; no life within, no warmth about her, and all my fancies were vain dreams. Then I buried my face in my hands, and wept as if my heart was breaking. And when I turned away my eyes from her, the presence came around me again. So long as I watched her, it was not there; I saw the corpse only; but when I shut this out from me, then it seemed as if a barrier had been removed, and that my sister floated near me again.

I had been praying, sitting thus in these alternate feelings of her spiritual presence and her bodily death, when, raising my head and looking towards the farther corner of the room, I saw, standing at some little distance, my sister Ellen. I saw her distinctly, as distinctly as you may see that red fire blaze. Sadly and lovingly her dark eyes looked at me, sadly her gentle lips smiled, and by look and gesture too she showed me that she wished to speak to me. Strange, I was not frightened. It was so natural to see her there, that for the moment I forgot that she was dead.

'Ellen!' I said, 'what is it?'

The figure smiled. It came nearer. Oh! do not say it was fancy! I saw it advance; it came glidingly; I remembered afterwards that it did not walk – but it came forward – to the light, and stood not ten paces from me. It looked at me still, in the same sad gentle way, and somehow – I do not know whether with the hand or by the turning of the head – it showed me the throat, where were the distinct marks of two powerful hands. And then it pointed to its heart; and looking, I saw the broad stain of blood above it. And then I heard her voice – I swear I was not mad – I heard it, I say to you distinctly – whisper softly, 'Mary!' and then it said, still more audibly, 'Murdered!'

And then the figure vanished, and suddenly the whole room was vacant. That one dread word had sounded as if forced out by the pressure of some strong agony, – like a man revealing his life's secret when dying. And when it had been spoken, or rather wailed forth, there was a sudden sweep and chilly rush through the air; and the life, the soul, the presence, fled. I was alone again with Death. The mission had been fulfilled; the warning had been given; and then my sister passed away, – for her work with earth was done.

Brave and calm as the strongest man that ever fought on a battlefield, I stood up beside my sister's body. I unfastened her last dress, and threw it back from her chest and shoulders; I raised her head and took off the bandage from round her face; and then I saw deep black bruises on her throat, the marks of hands that had grappled her from behind, and that had strangled her. And then I looked further, and I saw a small wound below the left breast, about which hung two or three clots of blood, that had oozed up, despite all care and knowledge in her manner of murder. I knew then she had first been suffocated, to prevent her screams, and then stabbed where the wound would bleed inwardly, and show no sign to the mere bystander.

I covered her up carefully again. I laid the pillow smooth and straight, and laid the heavy head gently down. I drew the shroud close above the dreadful mark of murder. And then –

still as calm and resolute as I had been ever since the revelation had come to me – I left the room, and passed into my husband's study. It was on me to discover all the truth.

His writing table was locked. Where my strength came from, I know not; but, with a chisel that was lying on the table, I prized the drawer and broke the lock. I opened it. There was a long and slender dagger lying there, red with blood; a handful of woman's hair rudely severed from the head, lay near it. It was my sister's hair! – that wavy silken uncurled auburn hair that I had always loved and admired so much! And near to these again, were stamps, and dies, and moulds, and plates, and handwritings with facsimiles beneath, and bankers' cheques, and a heap of leaden coin, and piles of incomplete bank notes; and all the evidences of a coiner's and a forger's trade, – the suspicion of which had caused those bitter quarrellings between poor Ellen and my husband – the knowledge of which had caused her death.

With these things I saw also a letter addressed to Ellen in my husband's handwriting. It was an unfinished letter, as if it had displeased him, and he had made another copy. It began with these words – no fear that I should forget them; they are burnt into my brain – 'I never really loved her, Ellen; she pleased me, only as a doll would please a child; and I married her from pity, not from love. You, Ellen, you alone could fill my heart; you alone are my fit helpmate. Fly with me Ellen – .' Here, the letter was left unfinished; but it gave me enough to explain all the meaning of the first weeks of my sister's stay here, and why she had called him villain, and why he had told her that she might tell me, and that I would not believe.

I saw it all now. I turned my head, to see my husband standing a few paces behind me. Good Heaven! I have often thought, was that man the same man I had loved so long and fondly?

The strength of horror, not of courage, upheld me. I knew he meant to kill me, but that did not alarm me; I only dreaded lest his hand should touch me. It was not death, it was he I shrank from. I believe if he had touched me then, I should have fallen dead at his feet. I stretched out my arms in horror, to thrust him back, uttering a piercing shriek; and while he made an effort to seize me, overreaching himself in the madness of his fury, I rushed by him, shrieking still, and so fled away into the darkness, where I lived, oh! for many many months!

When I woke again, I found that my poor baby had died, and that my husband had gone none knew where. But the fear of his return haunted me. I could get no rest day or night for dread of him; and I felt going mad with the one hard thought forever pitilessly pursuing me – that I should fall again into his hands. I put on widow's weeds – for indeed am I too truly widowed! – and then I began wandering about; wandering in poverty and privation, expecting every moment to meet him face to face; wandering about, so that I may escape the more easily when the moment does come.

THE SEVENTH POOR TRAVELLER
[by Adelaide Anne Procter]

We were all yet looking at the Widow, after her frightened voice had died away, when the Book Pedlar, apparently afraid of being forgotten, asked what did we think of his giving us a Legend to wind up with? We all said (except the Lawyer, who wanted a description of the murderer to send to the Police Hue and Cry,[77] and who was with great difficulty nudged to silence by the united efforts of the company) that we thought we should like it. So, the Book Pedlar started off at score, thus:

> GIRT round with rugged mountains
>   The fair Lake Constance[78] lies;
> In her blue heart reflected,
>   Shine back the starry skies;
> And watching each white cloudlet
>   Float silently and slow,
> You think a piece of Heaven
>   Lies on our earth below!
>
> Midnight is there: and silence
>   Enthroned in Heaven, looks down
> Upon her own calm mirror,
>   Upon a sleeping town:
> For Bregenz, that quaint city
>   Upon the Tyrol shore,
> Has stood above Lake Constance,
>   A thousand years and more.

Her battlements and towers,
　　Upon their rocky steep,
Have cast their trembling shadow
　　For ages on the deep:
Mountain, and lake, and valley,
　　A sacred legend know,
Of how the town was saved, one night,
　　Three hundred years ago.

Far from her home and kindred,
　　A Tyrol maid had fled,
To serve in the Swiss valleys,
　　And toil for daily bread;
And every year that fleeted
　　So silently and fast,
Seemed to bear farther from her
　　The memory of the Past.

She served kind, gentle masters,
　　Nor asked for rest or change;
Her friends seemed no more new ones,
　　Their speech seemed no more strange;
And when she led her cattle
　　To pasture every day,
She ceased to look and wonder
　　On which side Bregenz lay.

She spoke no more of Bregenz,
　　With longing and with tears;
Her Tyrol home seemed faded
　　In a deep mist of years,

She heeded not the rumours
　　Of Austrian war and strife;
Each day she rose contented,
　　To the calm toils of life.

Yet, when her master's children
　　Would clustering round her stand,
She sang them the old ballads
　　Of her own native land;
And when at morn and evening
　　She knelt before God's throne,
The accents of her childhood
　　Rose to her lips alone.

And so she dwelt: the valley
　　More peaceful year by year;
Yet suddenly strange portents,
　　Of some great deed seemed near.
The golden corn was bending
　　Upon its fragile stalk,
While farmers, heedless of their fields,
　　Pace up and down in talk.

The men seemed stern and altered,
　　With looks cast on the ground;
With anxious faces, one by one,
　　The women gathered round;
All talk of flax, or spinning,
　　Or work, was put away;
The very children seemed afraid
　　To go alone to play.

One day, out in the meadow
    With strangers from the town,
Some secret plan discussing,
    The men walked up and down.
Yet, now and then seemed watching,
    A strange uncertain gleam,
That looked like lances 'mid the trees,
    That stood below the stream.

At eve they all assembled,
    All care and doubt were fled;
With jovial laugh they feasted,
    The board was nobly spread.
The elder of the village
    Rose up, his glass in hand,
And cried, 'We drink the downfall
    'Of an accursed land!

'The night is growing darker,
    'Ere one more day is flown,
'Bregenz, our foemen's stronghold,
    'Bregenz shall be our own!'
The women shrank in terror
    (Yet Pride, too, had her part),
But one poor Tyrol maiden
    Felt death within her heart.

Before her, stood fair Bregenz;
    Once more her towers arose;
What were the friends beside her?
    Only her country's foes!

The faces of her kinsfolk,
   The days of childhood flown,
The echoes of her mountains,
   Reclaimed her as their own!

Nothing she heard around her,
   (Though shouts rang forth again,)
Gone were the green Swiss valleys,
   The pasture, and the plain;
Before her eyes one vision,
   And in her heart one cry,
That said, 'Go forth, save Bregenz,
   'And then, if need be, die!'

With trembling haste and breathless,
   With noiseless step, she sped;
Horses and weary cattle
   Were standing in the shed,
She loosed the strong white charger,
   That fed from out her hand;
She mounted, and she turned his head
   Towards her native land.

Out – out into the darkness –
   Faster, and still more fast;
The smooth grass flies behind her,
   The chestnut wood is past;
She looks up; clouds are heavy:
   Why is her steed so slow?
Scarcely the wind beside them,
   Can pass them as they go.

'Faster!' she cries, 'O faster!'
  Eleven the church-bells chime;
'O God,' she cries, 'help Bregenz,
  And bring me there in time!'
But louder than bells' ringing,
  Or lowing of the kine,[79]
Grows nearer in the midnight
  The rushing of the Rhine.

She strives to pierce the blackness,
  And looser throws the rein;
Her steed must breast the waters
  That dash above his mane.
How gallantly, how nobly,
  He struggles through the foam,
And see – in the far distance,
  Shine out the lights of home!

Shall not the roaring waters
  Their headlong gallop check?
The steed draws back in terror,
  She leans above his neck
To watch the flowing darkness,
  The bank is high and steep,
One pause – he staggers forward,
  And plunges in the deep.

Up the steep bank he bears her,
  And now, they rush again
Towards the heights of Bregenz,
  That Tower above the plain.

They reach the gate of Bregenz,
     Just as the midnight rings,
And out come serf and soldier
     To meet the news she brings.

Bregenz is saved! Ere daylight
     Her battlements are manned;
Defiance greets the army
     That marches on the land.
And if to deeds heroic
     Should endless fame be paid,
Bregenz does well to honour
     The noble Tyrol maid.

Three hundred years are vanished,
     And yet upon the hill
An old stone gateway rises,
     To do her honour still.
And there, when Bregenz women
     Sit spinning in the shade,
They see in quaint old carving
     The Charger and the Maid.

And when, to guard old Bregenz,
     By gateway, street, and tower,
The warder paces all night long,
     And calls each passing hour;
'Nine,' 'ten,' 'eleven,' he cries aloud,
     And then (O crown of Fame!)
When midnight pauses in the skies,
     He calls the maiden's name!

THE ROAD
[by Charles Dickens]

The stories being all finished, and the Wassail too, we broke up as the Cathedral bell struck Twelve. I did not take leave of my Travellers that night; for, it had come into my head to reappear in conjunction with some hot coffee, at seven in the morning.

As I passed along the High Street, I heard the Waits[80] at a distance, and struck off to find them. They were playing near one of the old gates of the City, at the corner of a wonderfully quaint row of red brick tenements, which the clarionet obligingly informed me were inhabited by the Minor Canons.[81] They had odd little porches over the doors, like sounding boards over old pulpits; and I thought I should like to see one of the Minor Canons come out upon his top step, and favour us with a little Christmas discourse about the poor scholars of Rochester: taking for his text the words of his Master, relative to the devouring of Widows' houses.[82]

The clarionet was so communicative, and my inclinations were (as they generally are), of so vagabond a tendency, that I accompanied the Waits across an open green called the Vines, and assisted – in the French sense[83] – at the performance of two waltzes, two polkas, and three Irish melodies, before I thought of my inn any more. However, I returned to it then, and found a fiddle in the kitchen, and Ben, the wall-eyed young man, and two chambermaids, circling round the great deal table with the utmost animation.

I had a very bad night. It cannot have been owing to the turkey, or the beef – and the Wassail is out of the question – but, in every endeavour that I made to get to sleep, I failed most dismally. Now, I was at Badajos with a fiddle; now, haunted by the widow's murdered sister. Now, I was riding on a little blind girl, to save my native town from sack and ruin. Now, I was expostulating with the dead mother of the unconscious little sailor-boy; now, dealing in diamonds in Sky Fair; now, for life or death, hiding mince pies under bedroom carpets. For all this, I was never asleep; and, in whatsoever unreasonable direction my mind rambled, the effigy of Master Richard Watts perpetually embarrassed it.[84]

In a word, I only got out of the worshipful Master Richard Watts's way, by getting out of bed in the dark at six o'clock, and tumbling, as my custom is, into all the cold water that could be accumulated for the purpose. The outer air was dull and cold enough in the street, when I came down there; and the one candle in our supper room at Watts's Charity looked as pale in the burning, as if it had had a bad night too. But, my Travellers had all slept soundly, and they took to the hot coffee, and the piles of bread and butter which Ben had arranged like deals in a timber yard, as kindly as I could desire.

While it was yet scarcely daylight, we all came out into the street together, and there shook hands. The widow took the little sailor towards Chatham, where he was to find a steam-boat for Sheerness; the lawyer, with an extremely knowing look, went his own way, without committing himself by announcing his intentions; two more struck off by the cathedral and old castle for Maidstone; and the Book Pedlar accompanied me over the bridge. As for me, I was going to walk, by Cobham Woods, as far upon my way to London as I fancied.

When I came to the stile and footpath by which I was to diverge from the main road, I bade farewell to my last remaining Poor Traveller, and pursued my way alone. And now, the mists began to rise in the most beautiful manner, and the sun to shine; and as I went on through the bracing air, seeing the hoar-frost sparkle everywhere, I felt as if all Nature shared in the joy of the great Birthday.

Going through the woods, the softness of my tread upon the mossy ground and among the brown leaves, enhanced the Christmas sacredness by which I felt surrounded. As the whitened stems environed me, I thought how the Founder of the time had never raised his benignant hand, save to bless and heal, except in the case of one unconscious tree. By Cobham Hall,[85] I came to the village, and the churchyard where the dead had been quietly buried, 'in the sure and certain hope' which Christmas time inspired.[86] What children could I see at play, and not be loving of, recalling who had loved them! No garden that I passed, was out of unison with the day, for I remembered that the tomb was in a garden, and that 'she, supposing him to be the gardener,' had said, 'Sir, if thou have borne him hence, tell me where thou hast laid him, and I will take him away.'[87] In time, the distant river with the ships, came full in view, and with it pictures of the poor fishermen mending their nets, who arose and followed him – of the teaching of the people from a ship pushed off a little way from shore by reason of the multitude – of a majestic figure walking on the water, in the loneliness of night.[88] My very shadow on the ground was eloquent of Christmas; for, did not the people lay their sick where the mere shadows of the men who had heard and seen him, might fall as they passed along?[89]

Thus, Christmas begirt me, far and near, until I had come to Blackheath, and had walked down the long vista of gnarled old trees in Greenwich Park, and was being steam-rattled,[90] through the mists now closing in once more, towards the lights of London. Brightly they shone, but not so brightly as my own fire and the brighter faces around it, when we came together to celebrate the day. And there I told of worthy

Master Richard Watts, and of my supper with the Six Poor Travellers who were neither Rogues nor Proctors, and from that hour to this, I have never seen one of them again.

THE END

NOTES

1. Sir Richard Watts (1529–79) established an almshouse on the High Street of Rochester, Kent that still stands and functions as an active charity, with its public rooms paying homage to Dickens' descriptions in this Christmas number. Kent, where Dickens passed some of his childhood, was one of his favourite regions, and settings in and around Rochester are central to *Great Expectations* (1861) and *The Mystery of Edwin Drood* (1870). Dickens visited Watts' Charity on 11th May 1854 and in 1856 bought the nearby Gad's Hill Place, a home he had coveted as a child and in which he died.

2. An official whose duties include attending to the church's interior.

3. Proctors, who solicited alms for lepers and other ostracised groups, were generally disrespected, and their reputations suffered further because they often took advantage of the proxy begging system.

4. King John of England (*c.* 1167–1216) reigned from 1199 until 1216 and is best known for sealing the first Magna Carta, which limited the powers of the monarch, in 1215, the year in which civil war led him to order a siege of Rochester Castle.

5. Mullioned windows use wide vertical bars or planks to separate the window into sections and are popular in Gothic architecture.

6. The court of the Lord Chancellor and the highest court next to the House of Lords, Chancery was infamous for its inefficiences in resolving common law disputes. Dickens satirically targeted Chancery in several works, including *Little Dorrit* (1855–7) and *Bleak House* (1852–3).

7. Referencing an essay in *New Monthly*, *The New Yorker* of 15th September 1838 (Vol. 5 No. 26 p. 408) finds convincing 'the circumstantial account of the huge oyster found on the coast of Massachusetts, the 14th of May, 1837, which was of such bulky dimensions, that, when removed from the shell, it required four men to swallow it whole!'

8. Spiced warm liquor drink traditionally used for Christmas Eve toasts and Twelfth Night celebrations, and made with various recipes, most including cloves, nutmeg, apples and ale. Exaggerating the narrator's ability to prepare the drink, the 'voice of Fame' phrase echoes Song of Solomon 2:12: 'The flowers appear on the earth; the time of the singing [of birds] is come, and the voice of the turtle is heard in our land.'

9. A frozen fog or mist.

10. A large drinking vessel or bowl; the term also refers to the vessel's contents.

11. An ostler was a stableman whose duties at the inn would be to care for travellers' horses.

12. The description 'wall-eyed' refers to strangely coloured eyes of various types, including very light, multi-coloured, or streaked irises, or eyes of different colours. A fly is a light, covered one-horse vehicle for hire; also called a hansom cab.

13. The nursery rhyme, first recorded in the early eighteenth century, actually describes the good fortune of Thomas Horner, a sixteenth-century steward who dipped into a pie containing hidden land deeds that he was supposed to deliver to King Henry VIII: 'Little Jack Horner,/Sat in the corner,/Eating his Christmas pie,/He put in his thumb–/And pulled out a plum/And said what a good/boy am I.'

14. See Luke 2:14.

15. Coloured ribbons bunched together to form cockades decorate military headdress and indicate allegiance. During the Napoleonic Wars (1799–1815), recruiting officers provided cockades to enlisting soldiers who responded to the shilling incentive.

16. Similar to solitary confinement, the punishment cell in a barracks.

17. A sometimes restrictive coat or marking on one's clothing to distinguish disfavoured, arrested or punished soldiers.

18. Presumably, the 'marks' and scars from flogging, a military punishment for disobedience.

19. Ancient Roman god of war.

20. At Trafalgar in southern Spain, the British naval fleet defeated the combined forces of France and Spain on 21st October 1805. Lord Admiral Horatio Nelson (1758–1805), who was already blind in one eye and missing one arm from previous battles, famously died at Trafalgar.

21. The Peninsular War took place for six years after the Spanish allied with the British to dethrone Napoleon's brother Joseph, whom he had installed as king following an 1808 victory; Britain aided Spain in reclaiming Badajos from the French in 1812.

22. In the final major battle of the Peninsular War, the Duke of Wellington led the British to victory at Toulouse, France on 10th April 1814.

23. See Luke 7:12 and following, in which Jesus encounters a crowd carrying a corpse at the gates of Nain ('there was a dead man carried out, the only son of his mother, and she was a widow') then reanimates the corpse to assuage the widow's grief.

24. See Luke 7:14.

25. Locations of the final battles of the Napoleonic Wars in present-day Belgium.

26. 'That rightfully famous man.' (French)

27. *The Arabian Nights* (also known as *One Thousand and One Nights*), a collection of Arabic tales dating from the eighth century that was in print in various translations throughout the nineteenth century, includes 'The Story of Aladdin and the Wonderful Lamp'. The saloon at the top of Aladdin's palace has twenty-four windows, all but one of which are full of rubies, diamonds and emeralds.

28. An axe-like wood-working tool with the blade at a right angle to the handle; its curve assists in cutting away the uppermost layer of wood.

29. Chatham's presence as a major British naval base dates to the mid-sixteenth century.

30. A screw ship is powered with a screw-propeller, multiple blades around a revolving central shaft close to the stern, and a blue-peter is a flag showing a white square in the centre of a blue field, which indicates the intention to sail immediately.

31. After 1807, when the British outlawed the trading of slaves (the practice of slavery itself remained legal in colonies), the navy patrolled the coast of Africa in an attempt to thwart persistent slavers – vessels carrying human cargo.

32. At the water's edge, the Common Hard is a street, strip or area of firm sand convenient for launching and landing watercraft. Able bodies, or ABs, and ordinaries are low-ranking merchant seamen.

33. Blocks are tree trunks or logs, and spars are long, pole-like pieces of timber.

34. Named for the origin of strong winds and storms, south-westers are waterproof caps with a neck covering usually made of oilskin. Guernsey shirts are knitted wool sweaters; the first ones made in England were crafted in the fifteenth century on the islands of Guernsey and Jersey in the English Channel.

35. In this context, if Acon-Virlaz purchases the debts, or 'acceptances', of the officers and pays the debts early, he will benefit from the discount received for early payment.

36. To crimp was to profit from trapping or forcing men into military enlistment.

37. Made of pilot cloth, a coarse, heavy blue wool usually used to make sailors' coats.

38. Eating a piglet would be offensive to Acon-Virlaz because consuming pork violates kosher rules.

39. Old Testament names used here as anti-Semitic monikers; Sheeny is derogatory slang.

40. A reddish quartz ring with a seal.

41. A decorated bottle or box with smelling salts or pungent liquids.

42. Sala's portrait intensifies the anti-Semitism of the story by describing Ben-Daoud using the most common anti-Semitic stereotypes.

43. See note 35 above.

44. Fungal infection of the mouth that produces white lesions, especially in infants.

45. A precious stone and gem crafter who cuts, engraves and polishes the stones.

46. A chaise or open, light carriage.

47. A supply delivery boat carrying meat and other perishables.

48. A policeman.

49. A weighted cord or rope used to establish a vertical line.

50. French term for an Indian dancing girl.

51. Based on circumstantial evidence, Ambrose Gwynnett was sentenced to death for murder, lay upon the gallows in chains, survived the hanging, and ultimately was rumoured to have met the person he had been convicted of killing.

52. This firework is named for St Catherine, who was tortured on a medieval spiked wheel. On the wheel, a person's crushed limbs were forced through the spokes and the still living victim was left hanging until they died.

53. Lying on the south bank of the Thames and now part of Southwark, Bermondsey was an area of ill-repute, and the oath 'Go to Bermondsey!' held a derogatory meaning close to the present-day 'Go to hell!'.

54. A worthless forged coin that had nevertheless functioned as currency in eighteenth-century Ireland because of its copper content.

55. Lithesome or supple.

56. Prepared a salted and smoked herring.

57. Willows used for basket-making because of their pliant yet durable branches.

58. When horses pull in tandem, the horses in front are the leaders and those following are the wheelers. The postilion is the rider of the leading horse, and seven-leaguers are of a very large size, alluding to the boots in the fairy tale 'Hop o' my Thumb' that magically gave the wearer the ability to cross seven leagues in one step.

59. Felt melancholy.

60. Wall supports made of stakes laced through with twigs.

61. Deals are long planks.

62. There is a billiard room. (French)

63. Rip Van Winkle, the eponymous hero of Washington Irving's (1783–1859) 1819 story, encounters strange, silent men playing ninepins and drinks their liquor before he sleeps in a wood then awakes to find that twenty years have passed.

64. A wooden shoe or clog, sometimes with a leather strip across the top.

65. Red or white wine from the Mâconnais region of southern Burgundy, France.

66. A high-quality lean French sausage that would have cost more than ordinary sausage.

67. A poplin-like fabric made of wool and silk with a watered pattern.

68. A *noceur* is a reveller. (French)

69. Elephantiasis is a skin disease that wrinkles and sometimes darkens skin, likening it to an elephant's hide; neuralgia causes nerve pain in the face.

70. Nasty or cruel. (French)

71. 'Pinxit' is a mark on a print indicating its original source, in this case probably Raffaelle Monti (1818–81), an Italian sculptor who moved to London in the mid-nineteenth century.

72. An 1829 melodrama by Douglas Jerrold (1803–57) in which a man is court-martialed for striking a captain who was trying to abduct his wife; the captain testifies that the husband's attack was justified.

73. Small woodwind instrument.

74. A character in the Handel (1685–1759) opera *Orlando* (1719), Medoro is an African prince usually played by a woman.

75. Fever.

76. A piece of cloth holding the mouth shut on a corpse.

77. A weekly paper established in the 1790s and later called *The Police Gazette* that reported and publicised information relating to crime and police affairs.

78. A lake in southeast Germany at the meeting point of Austria, Germany and Switzerland.

79. Mooing of the cow.

80. Public musicians usually playing woodwind instruments and especially active at Christmastime.

81. The clarionet is the player of the clarinet, and the minor canons are assistant, usually junior, clergymen at the cathedral.

82. In 1849, Rev. Robert Whiston began revealing that the Rochester Cathedral Chapter was misusing charity funds, particularly those intended for education, and the Biblical allusion to widows' houses refers to Mark 12:40, which warns against leaders who indulge selfish desires.

83. Witnessing or watching.

84. Impeded it.

85. A grand Tudor mansion in Cobham, Surrey.

86. References *The Book of Common Prayer*, 'We therefore commit his/her body to the ground;/earth to earth, ashes to ashes, dust to dust;/in the sure and certain hope of the Resurrection to eternal life' ('The Order for the Burial of the Dead').

87. Describing Mary Magdalene at Jesus' tomb, John 20:15 explains: 'Jesus saith unto her, Woman, why weepest thou? whom seekest thou? She, supposing him to be the gardener, saith unto him, Sir, if thou have borne him hence, tell me where thou hast laid him, and I will take him away.'

88. In his early ministry, Jesus climbs onto a ship that pulls a small distance from the shore in order to address a crowd more effectively. See Luke 5:1–3. Later in his ministry, Jesus walks 'on the sea' to meet disciples on board a ship. See John 6:16–19.

89. After Jesus' death, his disciples were thought capable of performing miracles, such as healing the sick. See Acts 5:15.

90. Jostled in a train with a steam engine.

BIOGRAPHICAL NOTE

Charles Dickens (1812–70), a true celebrity in the Victorian period, remains one of the best-known British writers. His most popular works, such as *Great Expectations* (1861) and *A Christmas Carol* (1843), continue to be read and adapted worldwide. In addition to fourteen complete novels, Dickens wrote short stories, essays, and plays. He acted on the stage more than once in amateur theatricals of his own production, and at the end of his life gave a series of powerful public readings from his works. Dickens' journalism is a lesser-known yet central aspect of his life and career. In 1850, he founded *Household Words*, where he worked as editor in chief in addition to writing over one hundred pieces himself. After more than twenty years of marriage, in 1858, Dickens abruptly separated from his wife Catherine in order to pursue a relationship with Ellen Ternan, a young actress. A dispute with his publishers, one of whom was representing Catherine in the separation negotiations, caused Dickens to engage in court proceedings over the rights to the name *Household Words*. As a result of winning the suit, Dickens folded *Household Words* into a new journal, *All the Year Round*, in 1859, with an increased focus on serialised fiction. From 1850 until 1867, Dickens published a special issue of these journals each December that he called the Christmas number. Collaborative in nature, including the work of up to nine different authors, the Christmas numbers were extremely popular and frequently imitated by other publishers. *The Seven Poor Travellers* is the first such number for which Dickens created a unifying theme, a narrative device that helped lead to the Christmas numbers becoming some of Dickens' most profitable endeavours, at times selling over 200,000 copies.

George Augustus Sala (1828–95), a prolific journalist and editor, was one of Dickens' protégés. After working as an illustrator and painter of theatrical sets, Sala turned to journalism in his early twenties. Many contemporaries noted the excellence of his first piece in *Household Words*, 'The Key of the Street' (6th September 1851), and Dickens' approval led to Sala's regular employment as a well-paid contributor. Dickens also edited Sala's pieces so heavily that many have misidentified some of Sala's writing as Dickens' own. Sala wrote for several important Victorian periodicals, including *The Illustrated London News*, to which he submitted the commentary 'Echoes of the Week' in 1862–7. He contributed to *The Daily Telegraph* for nearly three decades and travelled extensively throughout his career to write special interest pieces from Australia, northern Africa, Russia, and the United States. Sala published several collections of his journalism, such as *Twice Around the Clock* (1859), and wrote multiple novels, including *The Seven Sons of Mammon* (1862) and *The Strange Adventures of Captain Dangerous* (1862), which were published in *Temple Bar*, a liberal-leaning and respected periodical of which Sala was the first editor. Sala also co-authored a pornographic novel, *The Mysteries of Verbena House; or, Miss Bellasis Birched for Thieving* (1882). He was married to Harriett Elizabeth Hollingsworth in 1859; she died in 1885, and he married Bessie Stannard in 1890. Despite a successful career, towards the end of Sala's life he faced increasing financial difficulties as he struggled to balance what he referred to as 'bohemian' tastes with fiscal and professional responsibility.

Adelaide Anne Procter (1825–64) was a poet whose work earned admiration throughout Victorian society, from labourers to the middle classes to Queen Victoria. Procter was raised in a literary family, and her education at home and at Queen's College prepared her well for a life of letters. Because her father, Bryan Waller Procter (1787–1874), was friends with influential figures, such as William Makepeace Thackeray, Thomas Carlyle, and Dickens, Procter originally submitted her poetry to Dickens using the pseudonym Mary Berwick. She withheld her true identity from Dickens for over a year, and Dickens reflected on his own surprise in an introduction he penned for an 1866 edition of Procter's most famous verse collection, *Legends and Lyrics* (1858 61). In addition to frequently contributing verse to *Household Words*, Procter published in *The Cornhill* and was active in the Langham Place Circle, a group of progressive women activists. She cultivated close relationships with some leading feminist figures of the day, including Matilda Hays (1820–97) and the American actress Charlotte Cushman (1816–76), who lived in what was then termed a 'female marriage'. Procter agitated for education and employment equity for girls and women, founding the Society for the Promotion of the Employment of Women (SPEW) in 1859 with Jessie Boucherett (1825–1905). Before a protracted battle with tuberculosis ended her life, Procter completed *A Chaplet of Verses* (1862), which she published to assist a refuge for homeless women and children.

Wilkie Collins (1824–89) was an innovator in the genres of detective and sensation fiction and was one of Dickens' closest companions and collaborators. He published some of his most successful novels, including the phenomenally popular *The Woman in White* (1860) and *The Moonstone* (1868), in *All the Year Round* and sometimes managed the journal in

Dickens' absence. Collins and Dickens also collaborated on multiple theatrical productions, including *The Frozen Deep* (1857). Three Christmas numbers – *The Wreck of the Golden Mary* (1856), *The Perils of Certain English Prisoners* (1857), and *No Thoroughfare* (1867), contain only the work of Dickens and Collins, and *No Thoroughfare* was also a successful stage production. In addition to his work as a novelist and playwright, Collins found success as a journalist for several periodicals and wrote a well-received travel book, *Rambles Beyond Railways* (1851). Collins' best known work, *The Moonstone*, is one of the first detective novels in English and remains one of the most impressive examples of the form. His fiction often challenges nineteenth-century social convention, giving voice to characters with physical disabilities and advocating a subversion of many sexual norms. In Collins' personal life, he raised children with two women simultaneously, maintaining each in her own household and consistently opposing the institution of marriage.

Eliza Lynn Linton's (1822–98) mother died five months after Eliza's birth, and her father was an Anglican clergyman who rejected the notion that girls should be educated. She overcame her unhappy childhood by schooling herself in six languages and reading widely to become a groundbreaking Victorian journalist. Having already published extensively under her own name, Eliza Lynn, when she married William James Linton in 1858, she then appended his surname to her own. In 1848, Lynn became the first woman to be employed as a salaried writer by a periodical: *The Morning Chronicle*. She wrote for over thirty publications, including *The Cornhill*, *The Saturday Review*, *The Literary Gazette*, and Dickens' *Household Words* and *All the Year Round*. Although they did not always agree, Dickens respected her work highly, and she was a close friend of Dickens' sub-editor W.H. Wills as well as Walter Savage Landor. In 1856, she sold her house, Gad's Hill Place, to Dickens, who had admired the home since he was a boy. A complicated figure, Linton was independent in her own life, challenging many Victorian social mores and ultimately living separately from her husband. She wrote an essay complimentary of Mary Wollstonecraft, yet she was also an outspoken critic of what she called 'emancipated' women and early feminist movements. Linton is well known for 'The Girl of the Period' (1868), an unrelenting attack on the 'New Woman' that appeared in *The Saturday Review*. In addition to journalism, Linton wrote twenty-four novels, including *The Rebel of the Family* (1880), which features one of the first openly lesbian characters in English fiction.

Melisa Klimaszewski is an Assistant Professor at Drake University, where she specialises in Victorian literature, South African literature, and critical gender studies. She has published articles on nineteenth-century domestic servants and wet nurses, and she is now pursuing a longer project that focuses on Victorian collaboration. Author of the forthcoming *Brief Lives: Wilkie Collins*, she has edited several of Dickens' collaborative Christmas numbers for Hesperus and is co-author of *Brief Lives: Charles Dickens* (2007).

HESPERUS PRESS

Hesperus Press is committed to bringing near what is far –
far both in space and time. Works written by the greatest
authors, and unjustly neglected or simply little known in
the English-speaking world, are made accessible through
new translations and a completely fresh editorial approach.
Through these classic works, the reader is introduced to the
greatest writers from all times and all cultures.

For more information on Hesperus Press, please visit our
website: **www.hesperuspress.com**